The B.Y. Times

SUMMER DAZE

SUMMER DAZE

Created and written by
LEAH KLEIN

Targum/Feldheim

First published 1992

Copyright © 1992 by Targum Press
ISBN 0-944070-83-3

Phototypeset at Targum Press

Published by:
Targum Press Inc.
22700 W. Eleven Mile Rd.
Southfield, Mich. 48034

Distributed by:
Feldheim Publishers
200 Airport Executive Park
Spring Valley, N.Y. 10977

Distributed in Israel by:
Nof Books Ltd.
POB 23646
Jerusalem 91235

Printed in Israel

Contents

1. On the Road 7
2. Getting to Know You 17
3. Nechama's Find 26
4. Tryouts 31
5. Raizy's Offer 45
6. Night Stars 51
7. Friendly Sacrifices 61
8. Homecomings 75
9. Wounded Words 80
10. It's Only Fair 94
11. Soaring Free 106
12. *Camp Chronicles* 119
13. Mail Call 127

1
On the Road

The wide red and silver bus wound through the maze of city streets, traveled through the outskirts of the city, and finally headed for the highway. This early in the morning the road was quiet, but in the bus the sound of lively chatter filled the air. Girls called to each other across the aisles, laughing and talking, as they headed up towards the mountains for a summer in Camp Tiferes.

Raizy Segal stared out the window at the billboards rolling past. She brushed back a few straight, brown hairs that obstructed the view through her thick glasses, straightened her slightly stooped shoulders, and yawned. She and her friends had left Bloomfield early that morning to join the rest of the campers on the bus, and she still felt rather sleepy.

Raizy tried to swallow down the nervous feeling

that had settled at the bottom of her stomach that morning. New experiences were unnerving, she decided, and so were all these new faces. On the other hand, she reflected, just a year ago she would have never dared to try summer camp at all.

Raizy was only twelve, but she'd been skipped twice and had just graduated the eighth grade. Up until the beginning of the school year ten months ago she'd been a loner: the class brain with no friends. Then she had been appointed assistant editor of the new school newspaper, the *Bais Yaakov Times*. Working together on the six-member staff, shy Raizy had finally found her voice. The recognition she earned for her creative writing talents had given a much needed boost to her confidence. Best of all, her staff experiences had finally given her five real friends. And all of those friends were going to camp— together!

Shani Baum, seated beside her, was leaning halfway across the aisle, already engaged in a spirited conversation. Raizy smiled to herself as she observed her friend. Shani had been the editor of the *B.Y. Times*. Trust someone like Shani, vivacious and energetic, to dream up a newspaper in the first place. Already, Shani seemed to have made a new friend. Rina Waldman was her name. Tall and slim with dark, dancing eyes and wavy, short, black hair, Rina had a certain grace to her. By the looks of it, she was lively and popular with her friends. Not the type to be interested in quiet Raizy Segal, Raizy thought with a sigh.

The nervous bubbles settled as she found herself in the familiar position of sitting in Shani's protective shadow. Her behind-the-scenes position suited her. It was comforting to think of the summer following along this way. If things got too scary, if the crowds got too big, she could always count on Shani to be there. To be her friend.

The bus began its journey over a long, graceful bridge, leaving the smoggy city behind as it headed over the gray-blue waters.

Raizy turned her attention away from the scenery and back to the bus, where the girls' voices were growing louder and louder. Behind her, she could hear her friend Pinky speaking to a group of girls.

"Yes, we are identical," Pinky said. Pretty, with shoulder-length auburn hair and sparkling hazel eyes, Penina ("Pinky") Chinn turned to exchange a long suffering look with her twin sister, who was seated beside her writing notes in a yellow lined pad. Chaya Rochel ("Chinky") Chinn returned the look with a rueful grin. She was an identical copy of Pinky, but she wore her hair in a no-nonsense ponytail.

"Do you usually dress alike?" asked a slight, blue-eyed sixth grader, as she leaned over the back of her seat.

With a sigh, Chinky put down her pad and carefully put the top back on the pen. "Never. At least not since second grade."

"Except at our bas mitzvah," Pinky corrected her. "But that was special."

Their new friend looked disappointed. "I'd think it would be loads of fun. I've always wished I was born a twin."

Pinky adjusted her new barrette that held her hair. "Look, it's nice to be a twin — sometimes. But we're really two separate people, with different tastes."

Pinky was surprised at the sound of her own voice. It sounded like she was really uptight about this twin business. It usually didn't bother her too much when people asked the same dumb questions about being twins. But somehow she felt different about it today.

She thought about her unusual reactions for a minute and finally figured them out. She felt slighted! That was it! It was fine to be a cute twin when they were little, but now they were almost eighth graders; next year they would graduate! In school she was recognized as a person, as Penina Chinn — not just "one of the twins." She'd grown used to being accepted for herself, and she didn't relish the idea of giving up her identity, even if it was only for a summer.

And she wouldn't! She would be recognized for herself this summer...no matter what!

She heard Chinky patiently explaining that yes, they were identical and no, they never got themselves mixed up. Desperate to change the subject, Pinky turned to her ever-present sack of caramels. "Have one?" she asked.

Soon everyone was busy chewing the sticky sweets. Caramels were Pinky's biggest weakness. She carried a supply with her everywhere. A huge box of caramels took up a sizable amount of room in her luggage.

Pinky stared thoughtfully out the window. They were exiting the bridge now. Ahead lay the wide interstate parkway. She glanced at Chinky and smiled to herself. True, there were some disadvantages to being a twin, but in new situations like this one, it was very convenient to have her own lifetime best friend seated right beside her.

"How about one for me?" red-headed Nechama Orenstein broke into Pinky's thoughts. A year younger than the twins, Nechama had been one of the two sixth graders working on the *B.Y. Times* staff. "Please, pretty please, with a cherry on top," Nechama bent one knee and stretched out her hands in a theatrical gesture. The bus gave a sudden lurch as they hit a bump and Nechama tumbled forward into Chinky's seat. The girls roared with laughter.

"Okay, okay," chuckled Pinky. "You can even have two."

"Are sure you have enough to last the summer?" Nechama teased.

"Don't worry," said Chinky. "She's got enough to last through the winter. Just like a squirrel."

The bus's mike system suddenly squeaked to life. "Will the red-headed girl in the aisle please return to her seat." The bus driver momentarily focused on Nechama in his mirror.

Nechama hastily retreated to her seat beside Batya Ben-Levi. Dark-haired, brown-eyed Batya was the sixth member of the *B.Y. Times* and Nechama's classmate.

Nechama smoothed her frizzy red afro into place. She twisted open the caramel wrapper and offered the second one to Batya.

"No thanks," Batya said distractedly. She seemed intent on the view outside the bus window.

Batya doesn't seem to be her usual self, thought Nechama. She leaned across the aisle and tapped the girl in the next seat on her shoulder.

"Want one?" Nechama held out the wrapped caramel. A thin, dark-skinned girl stretched out her hand and smiled. "Sure, anytime! What bunk will you be in?" she asked.

Nechama handed over the candy with a flourish. "Juniors," she replied.

"Oh, I'm a senior," the girl said. "We'll probably be together for some activities though. They usually put the seniors with the juniors."

Nechama sat up straight in her chair. "Well, watch out for me when it comes to sports! I'm the Bloomfield *machanayim* champion!"

"Really?" The senior looked impressed. "We can use someone really good when it comes to playing against Camp Rina. We lose to them every year."

Nechama grinned and raised her arms in victory. "Camp Rina watch your step — Nechama Orenstein is waiting for you!"

Batya pressed her nose against the vibrating windowpane. At this point on the route the parkway ran through the edge of some small suburban towns. Looking closely she could actually see children playing in their large grassy back yards. It sort of resembled her own town of Bloomfield. Batya felt a prickle in her eyes.

She shook her head quickly. What was the matter with her? Batya had been to camp before, and she knew she was in for a great time.

It was just that — well — Batya tried to sort through her feelings. Partially it was wondering how Ima and Abba would manage the whole summer with their only child away at camp. Would they be lonely? And then there was Savta, the Ben-Levi's downstairs elderly tenant. Batya's constant visits meant so much to her. And lately Batya had spent a lot of time at the local nursing home. They too would miss her visits.

A little question mark crossed Batya's mind. Did it really bother her that they would miss her? Or was it, that she would miss feeling needed?

Batya felt the hot prickle again. She clenched her

teeth and stared hard at the scenery. This would never do! Determined to put herself in a better frame of mind, she turned to observe her fellow passengers.

Batya recognized the majority of the girls — her own Bloomfield schoolmates and many girls who had been to camp with her before. Still, there were quite a few new faces among the crowd. Batya's gaze fell upon a new girl sitting at the back of the bus. She had caught her eye even before the bus had driven away. Now why had she stood out among the others? Batya's brow creased in thought.

Oh! That was it. Batya had noticed her outside as they waited their turn to board the bus, because she walked with a noticeable limp and looked very unhappy.

Batya gave her a long sidelong look. She wore her hair in a short, blond pageboy, her eyes were green and deeply set. She would have been pretty — except for the sulky expression that marred her face.

On impulse, Batya tapped Nechama on the arm. "Nechama!" she whispered.

Nechama interrupted the animated sports conversation that she was carrying on. "Oh, Hello! I thought you were sleeping or something. What's up?"

Batya lowered her voice. "Do you happen to know which bunk the girl at the back of the bus is in?"

"The blond one? Her luggage was marked Tova Gutman — Juniors. That's our bunk."

"Really?" said Batya. Though she had wanted to

sound nonchalant, for some reason the news that this mysterious girl would be a bunkmate excited her.

Nechama eyed her suspiciously. "I don't get this — first you look like the world is coming to an end, now suddenly you're all excited."

"Just moody I guess," said Batya.

"Well snap out of it, Ben-Levi," Nechama said. "The only mood allowed in camp is a good mood!" She pointed out the window. "Look! We're almost there!"

The bus had taken Exit 23 off the main interstate, and was now traveling along Route 7. The road was narrow, bordered on both sides by rolling meadows. Tall, thick stands of pine, oak, and maple punctuated the wide open spaces. Purple-blue mountains swelled in the distance. The city seemed very, very far away.

Batya took it all in, but her thoughts went back to Tova Gutman. *The girl looks like she could use a good friend — and I plan to be the one.* Batya's heart lifted. *She would be needed in camp, too.*

"We're almost here! We're almost here!" The cry echoed up and down the bus as the girls crowded to the windows.

Slowly, the bus roared its way up the steep hill. They rounded a sharp curve and stared at the large, faded sign that hung over a wooden fence. "Welcome to Camp Tiferes," it proclaimed. The girls began to cheer. The bus swung into the narrow lane, leafy tree branches scraping at its roof. Loose gravel spurted around the big wheels as the bus came to a halt in the parking lot.

Stiff and cramped, Shani stretched in her seat. "We're finally here!" Excitement glinted in her eyes. She reached overhead and pulled down her jacket from the rack above. "Come on, Raizy, let's go!"

The bus doors opened with a bang. Fresh, country-scented air filled the bus. The girls filed down the aisle and quickly descended. Raizy inhaled deeply. That pure, wonderful country smell filled her with indescribable happiness.

Shani gave a little skip as they all made their way toward the main dining room. "Whoopee!! It's gonna be one fantastic summer!"

2
Getting to Know You

The girls scurried back and forth in their new home, a wooden bunkhouse with a cheerful red roof. The building bustled with activity as girls ran to and fro, choosing bunks and closet space and unpacking their luggage.

Batya watched as Tova awkwardly dragged her trunk toward the row of bunk beds parked along the wall. She hesitated and then approached Tova. "I'll push," she said with a smile as she bent toward the trunk. She gave a shove. The trunk moved and then came to a sudden halt.

Batya looked up in surprise. Tova stood before her, a frown on her face. "What do you think you're doing?" she demanded.

Batya straightened up. "I...I just wanted to help," she stammered.

"Well — don't," Tova said gruffly. With that, she turned her back on Batya and continued dragging her trunk along.

Batya stood still for a long moment. Then her mouth set in a firm line. She pulled her trunk out of the corner and set off after Tova.

Tova approached the last bunk bed, against the far wall, and stopped. Silently she bent to unlatch her trunk. Batya towed her trunk to the second to the last bed. She surveyed it with satisfaction. The narrow, flowered mattress didn't look too bad, and the top bunk was unoccupied. "Nechama," she called, "over here!"

Nechama pushed her trunk until it was beside Batya's. She groaned and rubbed her arms. "Why'd you have to come all the way down here?"

"It's a good spot," Batya said quickly. "You can have the top bunk."

Nechama arched her eyebrows in surprise. "Really," she muttered. After all their talk of taking two neighboring top bunks! "Just moody," Batya had said — well, BOY, was she ever!

Nechama shrugged and plopped down on her luggage with a thud. "Nuts! I hate unpacking. I'd love a good run around this place." She swung her legs hard against the side of her big, black trunk. "My legs are still cramped from that long bus ride."

"Let's start unpacking," Batya said quickly, taking an anxious glance at Tova. "This row of cubbies

must be for us. We'd better take the middle ones
while they are still available." She tossed her jacket
into one of the middle cubbies and proceeded to
unpack neatly folded piles of clothing onto her bed.

With her back to the two of them, Tova continued
unloading her trunk in sullen silence.

"What do you think we'll have for an activity this
afternoon?" Nechama asked, hardly noticing the quiet
girl standing next to her. Without waiting for a reply,
she went on. "Baseball! Now that would be the perfect
thing!" She swung an imaginary bat in the air. "Crack!
It's a hit, it's flying way overhead and Nechama
Orenstein is streaking past first base...."

"Nechama," Batya interrupted firmly, "when are
you going to unpack? We've only got until the lunch
bugle sounds. We've got to get these beds made up
by then."

Nechama sighed and arose from her trunk.
"You're ruining all the fun." She swung open the lid
of her trunk with a bang. "Guess I'd better get this
over and done with."

In the C.I.T. (counselor-in-training) bunkhouse
next door, Shani busily unpacked her trunk. Effi-
cient as ever, she stood back to admire her neatly
arranged cubby. "Done! Now for the bed — I de-
spise making these old hospital corners — might
as well get it done with. Want to see how it's done,
Raizy?"

Raizy looked up from her cubby where she was

meticulously refolding her nightgown. "What are 'hospital corners'?"

"That's the way you make up these narrow beds." Shani clambered up the side of the bed and spread her striped sheet over the top bunk. Standing on the foot of the lower bunk she proceeded to demonstrate the process of correctly tucking the sheet corners under the mattress.

"Hey, Rina, isn't this neat?" Shani proudly leaned back and surveyed her work.

Rina smiled. "It's gorgeous, Shani," she said. She slid her pillow into her pillowcase and tossed it up so that it landed on her top bunk.

Raizy gave her sheet a final pat. Done! It looked almost as good as Shani's right above her. She draped her quilt over the bed and fluffed her pillow up before laying it at the head of the bed. Raizy took a quick look at the other beds. Her flowered linens looked kind of faded next to the others, but Raizy didn't mind. Right now, the familiar bedding was a most welcome, homey spot in this new place.

Raizy sat down on her bed and began refolding some loose laundry that had come apart in her trunk. The buzz of conversation surrounded her. Laughter, giggles — everyone seemed to be having a good time getting acquainted. Why was it that at times like these she couldn't think of a single thing to say?

Usually, it suited her to be quiet. She wasn't the type that found it necessary to speak unless she really had something to say. But surrounded by the babble of voices, she just felt so conspicuous.

She could feel her face turning red.

Seated on the bunk above her, Shani was busy discussing something with Rina. Suddenly the springs creaked and sagged as Shani stood up on her bed. "Hey! Everybody! Look at this — this wall doesn't connect to the ceiling. Wait! Hand me another pillow to stand on, maybe I can see over the top. Yup! I can see straight into the storage room where they keep the luggage. How about it, Rina? We can have fun disappearing down there when the O.D.s (on-duty counselors) are on duty!"

Rina turned from her cubby and craned her neck to see. "It must be quite a drop. You'd need to get a ladder in there." She smiled. "You wouldn't want a pair of O.D.s carrying you directly to the infirmary."

Shani laughed. "I suppose you're right. Still, it was a good idea while it lasted." She carefully climbed down from her perch. "Are you almost done?" she asked Rina. "Let's DO something!"

"I've still got some straightening up to do," Rina replied. Shani wandered off to the front of the bunkhouse, looking around for new people to meet.

As she carefully hung her Shabbos dresses in a small closet, Rina turned to Raizy. "Is this your first time in camp?" she asked.

Raizy felt herself blushing. She sure can tell, she thought. "Yes," she said uncomfortably. Silently she folded the last items neatly together and placed the pile inside her cubby. She turned to leave the bunkhouse, itching to get away by herself for a bit, and explore the grounds.

Rina looked at her curiously. "Where are you going?" she asked.

Raizy gave her a surprised glance. She couldn't really be interested, she thought to herself. "Nowhere special," she replied and quickly left the bunkhouse.

Raizy left the cement path and walked through the grass surveying the bunkhouses that circled the grassy lawn. The bunkhouses were white with red roofs, and each had a narrow porch running the width of the building. She could see a small forest that bordered the camp on one side, and another circle of bunkhouses further on. Raizy walked toward the wide, tarred path that connected all the different parts of camp. Down the hill she saw the parking lot where her bus had left them off. The bus was gone, she noticed, already traveling back to the city. The thought made Raizy just a little bit homesick.

Raizy continued her walk. She saw well-tended flower beds near the dining room. The bright daffodils and petunias cheered her somewhat.

Still alone — the others were all finishing their unpacking — Raizy followed the path uphill. A little further ahead the path branched out. To her left stood the casino and swimming pool, to her right were the playing fields.

A thrill of happiness ran through Raizy — it was all so pretty, so pure and clean. On impulse, she gave a leap forward and ran as fast as she could through the fields. The breeze whipped through her hair, and she raced on, reveling in the peaceful freedom.

Pinky stood at her cubby happily shifting around the abundant piles of clothing. What a relief to get rid of that boring navy! With Pinky's artistic sense of color, being confined to a school uniform all year was absolutely stifling! Summer was her time to really let loose and enjoy the full spectrum of colors.

She looked down at her outfit with satisfaction. The dark green skirt that she wore matched perfectly with the green collar and cuffs of her bright yellow sweatshirt. The green and yellow stripes in her new hair clip really tied the whole outfit together.

Pinky groaned inwardly as she glanced at Chinky. How could she be wearing NAVY? It was a good thing they didn't dress alike, thought Pinky.

Chinky sat on her bed, scribbling something on a yellow legal pad. Her neat navy skirt was matched with a navy and white striped top.

"It's great having twins in our bunk," the girl on the next bunk bed remarked. "I mean it's like something different, y'know?"

"Yeah," a tall blond girl came to a standstill between the two beds. She looked from one twin to the other with interest. "I always wanted to be something different. When I was a kid, I wished I was a twin, then I wished I had freckles or red hair. Finally I convinced my mother and the eye doctor that I couldn't see well and I got a pair of glasses. I got tired of them pretty fast."

The girls hooted with laughter.

"But seriously speaking," she peered at them closely, "you two must be identical — you're exact copies!"

"Yup," said Chinky, "we are."

"Who's older?" she continued.

"Chinky is," said Pinky. "By a half an hour."

There was a little crowd clustered around the twins by now.

"I've got it!" someone exclaimed. "Identical twins are great for a good joke on the O.D.s! My sister once did it with the twins in her bunk. It goes like this...."

"Sorry, people," Chinky interrupted. "We're just not the type for twin pranks."

"Nope," Pinky added firmly. "Sorry." She quickly produced her sack of caramels from under her pillow. "Caramels, anyone?"

Chinky turned back to her pad. She hoped this would be the end of this twin fascination. It made her feel dumb. Besides, she noticed that Pinky was really getting upset with it.

Pinky walked toward the back of the bunk in search of the wastebasket. Disposing of her candy wrapper, she caught sight of her reflection in the full-length mirror on the wall. Pinky smiled, her mouth full of sticky caramel. She wasn't going to go for all of this "twin stuff." Nope. She liked being just who she was — Pinky Chinn.

The lunch bugle sounded from the office. The trumpeting sound floated up through the bunkhouses. It piped through the grassy fields and echoed against the mountains. Girls of all sizes streamed toward the path and headed downhill. The sound of rushing footsteps filled the dining room as each bunk took its place.

Batya looked hungrily at the pile of steaming cheese latkes in the middle of the table. It didn't look bad for camp food. Or maybe it was just that she was famished. It had been a long time since breakfast.

Nechama tugged at her sleeve. "Look that way, Batya." Batya followed Nechama's pointing finger. From the seniors table Chinky and Pinky were waving wildly in their direction. Batya grinned and waved back. She craned her neck in search of Shani and Raizy. There they were, at the corner table. She lifted her hands high and waved vigorously. They smiled and waved back.

Chairs scraped against the wooden floor, and silverware clinked against the table. That certain dining room din filled Batya's ears. A familiar feeling swept over her.

Camp had truly begun.

3
Nechama's Find

Crack! Bat met ball with a satisfying smack. Senior A groaned as Junior C scored a run. It was mid-morning, and the seniors were playing the juniors in an inter-bunk baseball game.

Batya squinted into the sun. She watched as Nechama came up to bat. It would be a while yet until her turn. She turned to observe Tova sitting at the sidelines — as usual. Despite the fact that she was capable of participating in most activities to some extent, Tova had made it clear from the start that she would have nothing to do with sports.

Batya sighed. Her repeated attempts to draw Tova into conversation had all met with the same rebuff — short, curt responses and stony silence.

Tova seemed to relax as she stretched herself out on the grass, head propped on one elbow. Her perpetual frown seemed to soften as she gazed off into the distance.

It seemed as good a time as any to try and break through the thick wall that Tova had built around herself. Batya slipped out of line and approached the prostrate girl.

"You're really tanning quickly — lucky you," Batya commented with a smile.

"Am I really?" Tova asked. A half smile snuck across her face.

Batya took a deep breath. So — Tova actually could smile! "Yep," she said aloud. "You look like you've been in camp for ages, not just a couple of days."

Tova pulled at some long blades of grass beside her. "Well, I do spend most activities sitting in the sun." That sad, sullen expression fluttered momentarily through her eyes.

"BATYA!" Her teammates called.

"Oops! See you!" Batya called over her shoulder, as she hastily raced up to bat.

Batya gripped the bat and stared ahead unseeingly. A little voice inside her whispered, "Tova's talking, Tova even smiled...."

She hit the ball and took off. She didn't get very far. A grinning senior tagged her before she even reached first base.

For some reason, she didn't mind. She glanced in Tova's direction, and Tova waved sympathetically.

Batya felt her heart give a little leap within her. Somehow, she was certain, Tova would yet be a friend.

Batya had given the juniors their third out, and the seniors came up to bat.

Pinky rubbed her sweaty palms against her skirt and adjusted the brim of her sun visor. The sun was beaming directly at her, as she stood poised and ready to run at second base.

Now it was Chinky's turn. Pinky watched as her twin came up to the plate. Chinky picked up the bat. The bases were loaded. The pitcher threw the ball. The auburn-haired girl swung the bat, and the ball soared high overhead.

"Let's go, Chinky — run!" her teammates yelled excitedly.

Chinky ran. Keeping one eye on the junior racing in the direction of the flying ball, she took off. Her sneakers pounded the ground as she raced around the baseline. Second base, third base — the junior with the ball was only a couple of feet behind her. Seniors and juniors held their breath. A burst of adrenalin, and Chinky bounced hard over home plate.

"Triple run!" The seniors were ecstatic.

"You did it, Chinky!"

"Good work!"

Flushed and panting, she grinned as her teammates surrounded her. "Chinky Chinn, at your service!"

"Okay, girls," their counselor interrupted. "Who's next up to bat?"

A senior stepped up to bat. Nechama squinted toward the plate from her position in the outfield. "Oh no!" she muttered to herself. She recognized this senior — she sure knew how to hit. Nechama braced herself to run.

Sure enough — there was the ball, streaking toward her! Nechama stretched to grab it, but the ball whizzed past her and landed at the edge of the woods that bordered the field. It bounced and rolled into the shrubbery. Nechama groaned as she raced furiously after it. It looked like the seniors would score another run.

She came to a short stop in the middle of the shrubbery. Where was that ball? She dropped down on her hands and knees and stretched her neck in all directions.

She peered under a bush and gave a little cry. A bright, beady pair of eyes stared at her. Startled, Nechama looked at the eyes' owner — a small brown bird. It seemed afraid of her, yet it didn't fly away. Instead, it gave a little backward hop, twittering in fright. One soft, brown wing dragged along the ground.

The bird was wounded. It couldn't fly. Poor little bird, it was probably starving, too. Slowly, Nechama stretched out her hands, and slid them under the bird, murmuring gently to it all the time. "Don't worry, little bird, I'm not going to hurt you."

The downy, warm little body flopped around in her palms as the frightened bird tried to find its footing.

"I'm not going to hurt you," Nechama murmured again and again. The little bird settled into her hands, cocking its head to stare warily at Nechama.

Footsteps crashed into the bushes around her. A bunch of breathless juniors surrounded her. "Nechama, what's happening? Where's the ball?"

Startled, Nechama looked up from the bird cradled in her hands. "Ball...oh, I dunno."

"What d'you mean? What are you holding?" they clamored.

"Shh — quiet! You're going to scare her," Nechama whispered. Murmuring softly to the bird, she walked away, heading for her bunkhouse.

The girls stared after her in surprise. "What in the world has come over Nechama?"

4

Tryouts

Nechama impatiently drummed her fingers on the table. Just this last song and they would finally be dismissed from lunch in the dining room. She couldn't wait to get back to her bunkhouse and check on the little bird nestled comfortably in the shoe box beside her bed.

Thump! Thump! Hands pounded the table, and the singing vibrated throughout the dining room. Nechama checked her pocket. The bread crusts she had taken were still there. At last the singing came to an end and *bentching* began. Before they had even finished, Nechama was on her toes, ready to get up and run.

Oh no! What was this? The head counselor was holding up her hand for silence. Nechama sat back resignedly on the bench with a sigh. Whatever it was, she hoped it wouldn't take long.

Chavie Fried, the camp's head counselor, blew hard on her whistle. The last murmurs quieted. The dining room was silent.

Chavie smiled broadly. "I'd like to make a couple of announcements before you are dismissed. First, we have an exciting event coming up in a few days." Chavie paused to heighten the dramatic effect, and then continued. "TRIP DAY!"

She gave another blast on her whistle. The swinging doors on either side of the dining room opened and two counselors roller-skated in. They reached the front of the dining room and unrolled a colorful poster.

A ripple of excitement ran through the dining room as the girls eagerly read the words written upon it: Mountainville Skating Rink, Here We Come!

Chavie waited for the cheering to subside. She gave a short blow on her whistle and smiled at all the excited faces. "And now for the second announcement — at the end of first trip, we will be having a banquet, which will include a cantata, performed by our campers. The cantata will include drama, choir, and dance. You may also join scenery and props committees. Tryouts will be held today during rest hour. Further information has been posted on the main bulletin board."

Pinky grinned at Chinky, seated directly across from her. "Scenery committee — did you hear?" Pinky asked. "I can't wait!"

"Take it easy, Pinks. You've got to get accepted first, you know," her twin teased her.

"You're just as excited as I am — and you know it!" Pinky retorted. "What are you going to try for? Drama? Choir?"

"You got it on the first try. I'm going for drama." Chinky pointed in Chavie Fried's direction and motioned for Pinky to be quiet.

Chavie threw up her hands. "And now, give me a 'T!' The dining room resounded with a rousing cheer.

"Seniors dismissed!"

"Juniors dismissed!"

Nechama flew from her seat. She raced to her bunkhouse and settled down on her bed with the shoe box on her lap. The little bird looked a little better today, she thought. The wing didn't seem to drag as much as it hopped around its cardboard home. She crumbled the bread into a corner of the box, and watched with satisfaction as the bird pecked at its meal.

Pinky strolled along the path leading to the senior bunkhouse, Chinky beside her. Everything around them seemed to wilt in the heat of the noontime sun. The bright yellow dandelions along the path were bowed over and shut, seemingly trying to escape the sun's powerful rays. The bushes and trees were still. Not a breeze rustled their leaves.

Pinky lifted her long, auburn ponytail off the back of her neck, and fanned herself vigorously.

"You're only going to make yourself hotter," Chinky commented. "You're burning more energy with all that fanning."

Pinky sighed. "I know, I know, but I can't help it." Suddenly she stopped in her tracks and stared down at the path. "Hey look! This path is actually melting from the heat!"

Chinky looked down at the tar path beneath her feet. The tar was sticky and wet looking. "You're right! Ugh! It's getting all over my sneakers."

Pinky pointed to a shady tree beside their bunkhouse. "I give up! Let's go collapse under that tree until it's time for tryouts."

Pinky stretched out on the grass, resting her chin in her palms. It was such a relief to get out of the glaring sun. She leaned her head on one hand and gazed upward at the canopy of leaves that were sheltering her. What a splendid combination of colors! Dark green, light green, chartreuse and emerald green all woven together with the golden thread of sunlight. The leaves formed a shady haven.

Thinking about colors brought the scenery committee back to mind. She wondered who would head the team. The thought of working under someone's direction brought a frown to her pretty face. She so loved the feeling of independence that she'd gotten as the art editor of the *B.Y. Times*. Pinky worked best when inspired by her own artistic visions. It just was so difficult to produce what someone else had dreamed up.

Pinky kicked at the grass with the toe of her sneaker.

"What are you grouching about, Pinks?" Chinky rolled over and faced her twin. "You're kicking up a lot of dust."

"I'm not in the mood for being on a scenery committee," Pinky complained.

"What do you mean? I thought you were dying to do it."

"Yeah, I am." Pinky hesitated. How to explain her feelings? "You see, Chinks, I don't just want to be on the committee. I want to head it. It's so stifling to work with someone else's ideas, when I have so many ideas of my own. It's like...like doing a paint by number!" Pinky plucked at the grass in disgust.

"You want to head it? So head it," Chinky said.

Pinky shook her head. "It's not so simple. I asked some of the older girls, and it seems that only staff members head the different groups and committees."

Chinky looked at her twin. "You can do it, Pinky. Anyway — it can't hurt to ask."

"D'ya really think so?" Pinky asked her twin with a sudden gleam in her eye.

"Why not? I have a lot of faith in you, sis. After all, you're the one who saved my election campaign. Remember?"

Pinky giggled. "Who can ever forget when we found all our posters drowning in bubble bath?"

Chinky gave her an answering grin. Now that the

election was over — with Chinky elected school president — she could afford to laugh at the disaster that had almost derailed her entire campaign.

Chinky rose and stretched out a hand toward Pinky. "Let's go in and have a snack before we go up to the casino."

Pinky grasped her arm and pulled herself up off the grass. The twins entered their bunkhouse together.

At the junior bunkhouse, Batya and Tova were walking up the steps, an uncomfortable silence between them.

The awkwardness had begun just after lunch, when Batya approached Tova as they emerged from the dining room with the crowd. A happy buzz surrounded them.

"Roller-skating...Trip...Tryouts...Drama...."

Batya was in high spirits. Tova had remained in a receptive mood since yesterday's conversation during baseball. She turned to Tova with a gleam in her eye. "Cantata is fun, Tova — we're going to have a great time!"

"We?" repeated Tova incredulously. "You must be kidding! I'm not going to be in it."

"Why not?" Batya dared to ask. "You can be in drama or choir or —"

"No, Batya," Tova quietly interrupted. "I just couldn't bear to be onstage and face a hundred pairs of eyes. I just can't...."

Batya had the urge to argue. Tova didn't have to stand in the first row, and even so, her limp was not that obvious. But for now she decided to just be glad that Tova seemed to be opening up and revealing the pain that was bottled up inside her. She would pursue the issue another time.

Without thinking, she hastily changed the topic. "Roller-skating is just a few days away — we'll enjoy that —"

Tova stared at her, as if she had gone out of her mind. "Roller-skating — I can hardly walk, remember? Do you expect me to go roller-skating?" Tova looked sullen again.

"Oh…" said Batya. "I forgot." The two trudged up the hill toward their bunkhouse in silence. Batya was lost in thought. She stared straight ahead. She had an idea. But would it work?

They entered the junior bunkhouse and found Nechama in her usual spot — right beside her feathered friend. Batya sat down beside her. "How's she doing?" she asked.

"Orenstein the Vet reporting," Nechama said, plucking an imaginary stethoscope out of her ears. She pushed a pair of pretend spectacles higher up on her nose. "Have you got any new patients for me? The hours at the clinic are from two to four. I accept anything that isn't vicious."

Her little act was received with laughter. "You're going to turn this place into a zoo!" someone called from across the room.

"If you bring anything on four feet into this room — I'm leaving!" a bunkmate said.

"Okay, okay," Nechama replied. "We'll restrict entrance to two-footed creatures."

"Seriously, Nechama, how's the bird doing?" Batya repeated.

"I really think she's getting better," Nechama replied. "Look, her wing isn't dragging as much."

"You'll have to put her in a better box then," Tova said. "You wouldn't want her to get loose in here, and hurt herself, before she's ready to be set free."

"To be set free..." Nechama repeated vaguely. She was surprised at how those words stabbed at her. It was funny how much this bird was coming to mean to her.

"You could use a big cardboard box with a piece of screening put over the open side," Batya said. She looked at her watch. "It's getting late. I'd better run to tryouts now. See you later." She grabbed her sun visor from her cubby shelf and hurried out the door.

She headed up toward the casino, where cantata tryouts were being held.

"Batya, Batya — wait for us!" Chinky and Pinky caught up with her as she turned onto the casino path.

"Hi, you two," said Batya. She looked fondly at her two friends. New friends are great, thought Batya, but there's nothing like old ones. Good old reliable friends.

"How's Nechama's bird doing?" Pinky asked.

"It seems to be improving," said Batya. "It's not surprising — with the kind of care Nechama is giving it. She hovers over it day and night, feeds it, and cleans its box."

"Really!" Chinky couldn't keep the surprise out of her voice. "Somehow, I never thought Nechama would be the type to play 'mother bird.' "

"Well, she is," Batya replied. "She doesn't seem to be playing either. She seriously seems to care about it."

"Well, Chinks, why don't we go check out this bird ourselves, after tryouts?" Pinky suggested.

"Good idea," Chinky responded as the trio stepped through the casino doors together.

The wood-paneled room was crowded with girls. The different cantata heads had each taken a corner to work in. Lines were forming in each corner. Girls of all ages chattered and giggled together. The canteen had opened during rest hour and crackling potato chip bags and popping soda tabs added to the noise.

Chinky got in line for dramatics. Simi, the dramatics head, walked over to her and gave her a gracious smile. "Oh great, I was hoping you'd come!"

Chinky looked puzzled. She wasn't all that great as an actress. "Me? Why?"

"You have a twin, don't you?" Simi continued enthusiastically. "We've got this great part for the two of you! It's gonna be just adorable — the audience will go crazy over it."

Chinky sighed and shook her head. This twin business again! "Sorry. We're not into that kind of stuff." She gestured toward Pinky, who had heard what was going on and had immediately come to stand beside her.

Pinky seconded her decision. "No, that's really not for us," she declared. "Anyway I'm not even planning on joining dramatics. I'm hoping to do scenery."

Though she kept her voice calm, Pinky felt very annoyed. Twin, twin, twin! Enough already! Didn't anyone see them as two separate people? It was as if Pinky didn't count on her own. It was like being some kind of half-person. Well, she was determined. Maybe if she would get the chance to head the scenery committee, people in camp would see her differently...as a real, whole, separate individual. As herself!

"Look," Simi continued. "You can still do scenery. The part that we have planned for you doesn't take much practice. You see, we wanted you to represent happiness and sadness, in the form of two identical clowns."

Chinky and Pinky looked at each other. "What do you say, Pinks?" Chinky asked, with a slight shake of her head.

Pinky looked determined. "The last time Chinky

and I dressed alike was at our bas mitzvah party. The very last time. We're two different people with different talents. We just can't do it."

"Oh come on..." the dramatics head said, looking very disappointed.

Chinky shrugged her shoulders. "I'm really sorry."

"Sorry," Pinky echoed. She walked off in search of the cantata director to speak to her about scenery.

The dramatics head turned back to her script, and tryouts proceeded. Chinky breathed a sigh of relief as Simi gave her attention to the other girls.

Pinky spotted Faigy, the head of the entire production, standing on the other side of the room. She was rushing from corner to corner in the large casino. She looked important and busy. Pinky felt silly. After all, the head of scenery had probably been appointed already. "It can't hurt to ask," a small voice said inside her. Gathering her courage she crossed the room.

"Excuse me," she said. "I would like to speak to you about the scenery committee."

Faigy looked at her distractedly. "Scenery committee, right? Well let me write your name down on the list. I'll be checking into it later on when I've finished organizing the other committees." She dug her pen out of her pocket. "What's your name?" she asked hurriedly.

Pinky opened her mouth to answer. "This is your chance, ask about heading it," the little voice said inside her. "Are you a whole person, or are you not?"

Finally, the words came out in a quiet voice that Pinky hardly recognized. "I, um, I wanted to know about heading the committee," she said.

Faigy looked up from her notebook. "What did you say?"

Pinky swallowed. "I want to apply to head the committee," she said.

Faigy looked her up and down with interest. "Well, we actually don't have a head, as of yet, but you are rather young to head the committee. There is a lot of responsibility involved. Have you ever worked on a project of this sort?"

"I was art editor of my school newspaper this year, and I've worked on some other art projects at school," Pinky said hopefully. "And I made the art project for our regional Bais Yaakov convention."

So they didn't have a head yet! Maybe her dream would come true after all. Maybe....

"Faigy!" someone called from across the room. "We need you!"

Faigy turned to Pinky. "I'll have to think about this. Now let me write down your name."

"Penina Chinn," said Pinky.

Faigy jotted it down in her notebook. "Penina Chinn," she repeated. "Oh, one of the Chinn twins, right?"

"Penina Chinn," she repeated firmly, as Faigy capped her pen and hurried off.

In the senior bunkhouse, all was quiet. The majority of the girls, Shani among them, had rushed off to cantata tryouts.

Raizy yawned contentedly. Camp was beginning to feel more like home, yet she found the sudden privacy very welcome. She adjusted her pillow to a more comfortable position behind her, and continued scribbling in her notebook.

Dear Tatty and Mommy and Everyone,

How are you? I hope this letter finds everyone well, and enjoying their summer.

I am fine, B"H. I am starting to get used to camp. Our counselors are fantastic, and the kids in my bunk are very nice, too. I haven't gotten to know any of them very well yet. I love the camp grounds! They are spacious and beautiful. There is plenty of room to run around and all kinds of new flowers and trees to learn about. There is a lot of singing, yelling, and cheering that I don't care for, but I guess I'll get used to it.

Yesterday, we had —

Raizy started in surprise. What was that announcement coming over the mike? Was it her own name she had just heard? The mike crackled to life again.

"Raizy Segal, Raizy Segal — to the staff dining room."

There was no mistaking it. Raizy jumped out of bed, her mind in a whirl. Who could be waiting for her in the staff dining room? What was this all about?

Raizy stuck her feet into her sneakers and tied them tight. She hurriedly slipped her notebook under her pillow and gave her cover a quick pat.

Taking a deep breath, she set off in the direction of the staff dining room.

5
Raizy's Offer

Raizy paused before the double doors of the staff dining room. What was waiting for her on the other side? she wondered.

Finally, she pushed open the door and entered. At the far end of the dining room, Chavie Fried sat at a table, writing something down on her clipboard. She looked up, smiled, and motioned for Raizy to come over to her.

"Hi! How are you, Raizy?" she asked warmly.

Raizy felt herself blushing. "Fine," she said awkwardly. What a silly answer, she thought to herself, turning even redder.

Chavie adjusted the hair band that held back her thick, dark hair. "I've heard that you are a talented writer, Raizy," she said. "I understand that you headed a school newspaper this year."

"I was only assistant editor," Raizy said. She wondered what Chavie could be leading up to.

Chavie smiled. "Very modest — I like the combination of talent and modesty. You must be wondering what this is all about. It's like this. We would like to put out a camp newspaper. It would be published at the end of each trip, in time for the banquet. A newspaper can kind of sum up the trip, and in addition, it would give the campers something meaningful to take home. Kind of a souvenir of their summer in camp."

Raizy nodded her agreement. It made sense. But what did this have to do with her?

Her tension eased somewhat. The head counselor's way of talking directly to her, almost as if they were friends, made her feel a lot better.

Chavie leaned back in her chair, put down the clipboard and looked Raizy squarely in the eye. "We would like you to head the publication. I am convinced that you have the talent and experience to be the ideal person for the job."

Raizy felt a combination of surprise, delight, and embarrassment all mixed together.

"Me? Really?"

"Yes you. Really!" Chavie replied with a grin. "Do you accept?"

Raizy's brain whirled. Accept? Accept a dream come true?

"Sure! Of course! With pleasure!"

Raizy glowed with happiness. Me! They chose ME! The words sang inside her head. So many, confident, witty girls — and she was the one picked!

She wondered if Chavie knew how much it meant to her.

The head counselor was speaking. Raizy forced herself to focus on her words.

"Good. We were hoping you would." Chavie picked up her clipboard and pen in a businesslike manner. "Okay. Let's get down to details. There's too much work here for one person, that's for sure. You'll need someone to work with. I suggest you pick an assistant editor. I leave it to your discretion — just be sure to pick someone you can work with."

Shani automatically came to Raizy's mind. Who else? What fun they would have putting out a newspaper — together! It would be just like the *B.Y. Times*....

"Yes. I'll take care of that," she said aloud.

"Here is a list of topics that we would like included in the newspaper. You can come up with a format of your own," Chavie proceeded.

Raizy nodded. "No problem," she said.

"You'll need a place to work," Chavie went on. "You can work in the staff dining room during rest hour. It's vacant then. The office staff will run off the paper for you, and you can get a crew together to collate it."

She consulted her clipboard. "All articles are

subject to my approval. Please get back to me by the end of the week with your choice of assistant and a newspaper format."

Chavie stuck her pen back into the holder she wore around her neck. "That's it then. Any questions?" She gathered her things from the table.

"When's the deadline?" Raizy asked, trying to duplicate the head counselor's businesslike tone.

"We will be giving it out at the banquet. The newspaper should be ready to be run off four or five days in advance. That gives you three full weeks." Chavie stood up and straightened her skirt. "Okay then?"

"Yes — and thank you." Raizy found herself reddening once more.

"Lots of luck."

Raizy walked, or practically skipped, out of the dining room. Entering the still quiet bunkhouse, she drew out her notebook from under her pillow. She sat down on the edge of her bed and continued her letter.

Guess what? The head counselor just asked me to head the camp newspaper! I'm so excited!

"What's up?" Shani's voice broke the silence of the empty bunkhouse. "I heard you being paged during cantata tryouts and came back here as soon as my turn was over. Is everything all right?"

"More than all right. It's great news," Raizy reported happily. Her words poured out in one breathless tumble. "Chavie Fried asked me to head the camp newspaper. She told me to pick an assistant — of course I choose you."

Shani stared at Raizy wordlessly. Assistant? Assistant to Raizy? Quiet, shy Raizy Segal, whom no one had ever noticed until she had joined the *B.Y. Times* — Shani's newspaper! Ridiculous! Why, it was...it was just insulting! Who did Raizy think she was, anyway?

Her pink cheeks burned scarlet. "Sorry, Raizy," she snapped. "I'm...I'm way too busy. You'll have to choose someone else."

Raizy felt a sharp needle rip through her happiness. Shani wasn't happy for her. In fact, she looked downright angry.

Raizy hesitated, wondering what to say to calm down her friend. The bunkhouse door opened, and in walked Rina Waldman. Pointedly turning her back on Raizy, Shani gave her a bright smile. "Hi, Rina. Did you get your turn? Seems like the whole camp wants to be in cantata!"

Rina laughed merrily. "It was fun watching everyone try out. I hope we make it." She put her clogs back into her cubby and stuck her feet into sneakers. "They said that the different groups would be posted on the bulletin board after lunch on Wednesday."

Without a glance in Raizy's direction, Shani walked over to the mirror and ran a brush through her tight blond curls. "Wednesday? I was hoping they'd announce it at night activity."

The bugle sounded, announcing the end of rest hour. Shani put down her brush and walked toward the door. Rina followed right behind her.

"Coming, Raizy?" Rina called over her shoulder.

"In a minute. I just have to finish this letter," Raizy answered.

"Yeah," said Shani bitterly. "Raizy's a writer." And she walked out the door without a backward glance.

Raizy sat still for a minute, weighed down with misery. She hadn't dreamed that Shani would react this way.

There was still her letter to finish and send out. Dejected, she picked up her notebook.

No more news now. More next time.

Love, Raizy

Dragging her feet, she headed for her next activity.

6
Night Stars

The casino was filled to capacity. Each bunk sat on its assigned bench waiting for the stage curtains to part. The lights dimmed. A pink spotlight cast a bright spot on the dark curtains. Chavie Fried parted the curtains and stepped forward into the circle of light.

Shani leaned forward and strained to see over the girls seated on the bench in front of her. Night activity was her favorite camp activity. The competition and excitement were just right for Shani.

Chavie blew sharply on her whistle, and the casino magically became silent. "Tonight's night activity is...." A dramatic pause. "The activity for to-night is... TWENTY QUESTIONS!!' "

Loud applause followed. "Twenty Questions" was a camp favorite. The curtains were drawn aside, revealing four chairs set up in the middle of the stage.

Chavie proceeded to announce the onstage contestants. "...And, representing the C.I.T.s — Shani Baum!"

"Shani, Shani — let's go, Shani!" The C.I.T.s cheered loudly for their popular bunkmate, sure she would do them proud.

Shani beamed with delight. She hurried up to the stage, cheeks flushed, eyes shining with pleasure. Raizy watched as the four contestants took their seats amidst much cheering.

A large placard was presented to the audience. The name "Mr. Grundswieg" was stencilled upon it.

Shani was the first to ask her question. She stood up confidently. "Is it a person?" she asked.

Her bunk's loud cheer answered her question. "Shani, Shani, Shani!" they cried, elated.

Shani beamed down from the stage. Her blond curls, looking like a halo around her face, magnified her glow.

Because she got the first question right, she continued her turn.

"Is it a person in camp?" she asked.

"Shani, Shani, does it again!" the C.I.T.s chanted ecstatically. Shani clenched her fists tightly at her sides. Could she possibly win this round in one shot?

"Is it a woman?" she asked.

"No. It's not." Chavie Fried announced. Shani smiled at the audience — she was no sore loser! — and sat down on the edge of her chair, waiting for her turn to come up again. Squinting, she could make out her bunk, seated on their bench. She sought out Raizy to exchange a victorious look. Suddenly she remembered their conversation that afternoon, and how stricken Raizy had looked. Filled with the good-will of her triumph, she decided to apologize for her manner of speaking that afternoon. Maybe she had been a little harsh. But she definitely wouldn't accept the position of assistant to Raizy. She shook her head slightly. No, it just wouldn't do.

Where was Raizy, anyway? Shani blinked and stared hard into the dark casino. She couldn't find her. Oh well, she would see her later, she decided, after night activity.

Raizy sat in the grass outside the casino, her arms wrapped around her knees. Sitting in the semi-dark casino, remembering her conversation with Shani, her head had begun to ache. Suddenly the noise and commotion in the room overwhelmed her. With a quiet word of explanation to her counselor she left the casino and wandered outside into the cool night.

Raizy rested her forehead on her knees for a moment. What a relief the peaceful darkness was! She lifted her head and gazed upwards at the starry night sky. Stars had always fascinated Raizy. They were so beautiful and so mysterious. She had read up on the different constellations, and her knowledge made the sky even more exciting.

The velvety night sky was undisturbed by city lights, and in the pitch blackness the stars glowed luminous and bright. Raizy could make out the more familiar patterns. There was the Big Dipper, with the Little Dipper glittering opposite it. A faint light flickered in the blackness and then disappeared: a shooting star, perhaps, or a small plane?

Raizy started in surprise, as someone suddenly sat down beside her in the grass.

"Rina," she gasped. "Wow, you scared me."

"I saw you leaving and was wondering where you had disappeared to," Rina said. "What are you doing out here?"

Raizy reddened with embarrassment. What was she going to tell Rina? That she was miserable because her best friend was angry with her? That she had come out to enjoy the quiet beauty of the stars? She'd think she was crazy!

"I'm just...stargazing, I guess. I've done some reading on the different constellations, and this is a great spot to observe them from," she finished lamely.

"Can you really recognize the different constellations?" Rina asked with interest. "I always love to watch the stars, but I don't know much about them."

"I don't know that much about them, but I can show you a few of them." Raizy pointed her finger just above the distant tree line. "If you look closely, you will be able to make out seven bright stars in the shape of a dipper. Those are the constellation of Ursa Major."

Rina followed her pointing finger. "Which way does it go? Oh, now I see it! It really does look like a dipper."

Rina really seems genuinely interested, Raizy thought. She had never had anyone to share this with. Her misery somehow had disappeared, and she felt happy inside.

"Uh-huh, that's why it's called the Big Dipper. Opposite it, you can see the seven stars of Ursa Minor, which form the Little Dipper. See that especially bright star at the tip of the handle? That's the North Star. The northern end of the world's axis points toward it." Raizy traced the pattern, her finger stabbing the night air.

"It's really fascinating," Rina commented. "What's that little cluster of stars called?"

"The nickname for that one is the Seven Sisters. See how they are really seven little stars, all stuck together?"

"You really know a lot about the stars." Rina was impressed.

"It's just some information that I picked up from a library book." Though she tried to keep her voice nonchalant, deep down, Raizy was pleased with the compliment. "When I'm interested in something I always like to read up on it, and astronomy is pretty fascinating. But I love the stars for their own sake. There is something so awesome about them."

Rina nodded slowly. "They make me feel very small."

She understands, thought Raizy. "Yes," she said aloud. "It's a good reminder of the bigger things in life and what great things Hashem created."

There were a few moments of silence as the two girls gazed upwards.

Raizy broke the spell. "Do you know that the summer is actually the best time to watch the stars, though August is better than July," she said.

"Why's that?"

"Because the peak season for shooting stars is August through September," Raizy answered. "I think I may have seen one right before you joined me. Even now, you can see one if you're patient."

"Really! Are they colorful?"

Raizy smiled at Rina's excitement. "Not really. All you see is a blazing whoosh for a moment. But it's kind of exciting. And there's a special *berachah* to make on one."

"I'd love to see one!" Rina stared upward. "Let's be quiet and wait."

Raizy laughed. "The stars don't need quiet. You just have to watch long enough."

Back in the casino, the game was drawing to its conclusion. It was Shani's turn again. Her eyes were squeezed tightly shut as she racked her brain. Who could it be? All of the men on the camp staff had already been named. Suddenly a picture of the handyman flashed through her mind. "Is it... is it... Mr. Grundsweig?"

"Shani, Shani, Shani!" the C.I.T.s cheered loudly. "C.I.T.s do it again!"

Flushed and happy, Shani stepped off the stage. She made her way through the throng of girls gathering around her. A quick check through the bunk and she soon saw that Raizy was not in the casino.

Shani grew worried. Was Raizy so upset that she had remained in the bunkhouse, alone?

When the camp was dismissed, Shani hurried toward the casino exit with the rest of the crowd. She quickly turned up the path leading to their bunkhouse, determined to find Raizy and apologize.

Suddenly she caught sight of two figures sitting in the grass, their backs turned to the casino. Shani stopped in her tracks and stared. Who could be sitting in middle of the field at this hour? Wait — was that Raizy?

It was. Her eyes adapted to the dark, and she could make out Rina and Raizy absorbed in conversation.

A bitter feeling welled up in Shani's heart. So that's where my friends were — while I thought they were sitting and cheering for me onstage. And since when do Raizy and Rina have so much to talk about? I wonder what they're discussing together. Probably the way I rejected the newspaper offer!

Suspicion quickly painted a nasty picture in her mind. She imagined her two friends sitting and discussing her. Shani walked on alone, downcast and angry. Gone were any thoughts of apologizing to Raizy.

The hour grew late and nighttime settled over Camp Tiferes. The moon shone and the stars twinkled knowingly, casting their silvery light over the mountains. The fields and paths, teeming with activity by day, were silent. Even the red-roofed bunkhouses were quiet at last. Only the soft sound of peaceful breathing punctuated the darkness.

But not everyone was sleeping. Raizy lay on her bunk staring at the mattress above her. What a confusing day it had been. She tried to sort through the turmoil of confusion in her heart.

Elation rushed through her as she thought of her conversation with Rina. Rina was really interested in her and her ideas. Imagine! Popular, confident Rina interested in what Raizy Segal had to say! The thought sent all kinds of ideas through her mind. Perhaps other girls saw her that way, too. Maybe she wasn't such a bore after all. Was it just her own shyness that made her feel so awkward at times? All kinds of exciting possibilities flashed through her mind, as she restlessly tossed about on the thin mattress. After all, why should she feel like such a failure? Look at the friends she'd made this year working on the *B.Y. Times*.

The *B.Y. Times*. Shani.

When she thought about Shani, her heart plummeted. Her best friend. How could this have happened? She wished Shani would at least speak to her, so they could talk it out. But tonight, after night activity, Shani had ignored her completely. She'd pretended not to hear her when Raizy asked if she could speak to her.

Raizy felt like a kite on a windy day, tossed from one extreme to the other. Happy and excited for a moment and then suddenly sad and depressed. Twisting and turning, she finally dozed into a fitful sleep.

In the junior bunkhouse someone else was keeping a night watch. Pinky looked at her luminous alarm clock. Ten-thirty. She sighed as she glanced at her sleeping twin in the next bunk. It wasn't that she wasn't happy to have been born a twin. No. Not at all. Having a twin was a unique way of being linked with somebody for life. There was a special bond between them that Pinky wouldn't have traded for anything. And she loved Chinky dearly. She thought fondly of all the memories they shared. Growing up together. Learning and laughing together.

But, this summer was different. Suddenly she felt a need to prove herself. To be a person on her own. A strong need. She knew that Chinky felt it, too. It was like an unspoken agreement between the two of them: this summer we are not going to be "the twins."

No one else seemed to notice. "One of the twins,"

the tag followed them around like a pesky fly. And now here was the perfect opportunity to prove herself. If only she could persuade Faigy to let her head the scenery committee. It would be her chance.

Pinky thought it over. She couldn't just sit and wait for a refusal. She had to do something. But what?

Perhaps she should draw or paint something to show Faigy. She turned over the idea in her mind. Not bad. Suddenly Pinky remembered. Tomorrow was Trip Day. There would be no rest hour to work on a project.

As much as Pinky loved to skate, her decision was instantaneous. She would stay behind and work on her project. Her mind made up, a plan of action at hand, Pinky relaxed at last.

She smiled sleepily. Even if nothing came of it, she happily anticipated having a day to spend on an art project. Come to think of it, with a whole day to spend she could really produce something magnificent. Colors and scenes danced before her tired eyes, as ideas appeared in her mind. The colors of reality faded. The pretty, auburn-haired girl slept at last, a rainbow of hues coloring her dreams.

7
Friendly Sacrifices

C hinky felt someone shaking her out of her deep sleep. Her eyes flew open.

"What's going on?" she cried in alarm.

There, above her, she saw...was it her own reflection? Was she dreaming?

She rubbed her eyes. That was better. No, it wasn't her own reflection standing over her. It was Pinky, dressed in her white and orange flowered nightgown, sleep-tousled hair falling all over her face.

"What's the matter?"she asked, fully awake now.

"Shh!" Pinky put a finger to her lips. "Nothing's the matter."

"Nothing's the matter?" Chinky stared at her twin as if she'd gone out of her mind. "If nothing's the matter, why are you waking me up in the middle of the night?"

"Calm down, Chinks. It's not the middle of the

night. The wake-up bugle is going to ring in a half an hour. I just needed to talk to you." Pinky smiled to herself at the irony of the situation. Here she was, up at the crack of dawn in search of independence, waking up Chinky because she had to talk to her!

Chinky rose sleepily from her bed and washed her hands. In a few minutes she was back, perched on the bed beside Pinky. "So what's up?" she asked.

"It's about heading scenery. I thought of a way of proving my ability to Faigy. I've decided I'm going to do some kind of art project for her. I have to do it today. So I guess I'm going to miss the trip."

Pinky watched for her twin's reaction.

Chinky looked at her searchingly. "Miss the trip? Are you sure it's worth it?"

"I've decided. I really want to do this," Pinky said firmly. "Now that I'm going to have the whole day to spend, I can do a real project. Only problem is—what type of project do you think I should do?"

"Project? Let's see. You could make a sign on just about anything for the dining room or lobby. You know, use a *pasuk* or a *chazal* or something from this week's *Pirkei Avos*."

Pinky drew her feet up under her pink flowered nightgown and wrapped her arms around her knees. She rested her chin on her knees, brow puckered in thought. "Sign for the dining room or lobby... *Chazal*, *Pirkei Avos*... Ugh! It's so unoriginal. The walls are just covered with them."

"Anything you do is going to stand out, Pinky." Chinky sounded very sure of herself.

"Maybe. But I want to do something really striking. Something that will make Faigy say, 'We want Penina Chinn to do scenery.' "

The two girls sat, side by side, concentration written all over their faces, looking rather like a double exposure.

"How about something for the camp?" Chinky mused.

"Like what?"

"Like an *al hamichya* plaque for the snack area, or, say, a sign listing the phone hours for the pay phone."

Pinky sat up straight. "Now that's an idea! Something for the camp to use...."

The bugle sounded, its blast penetrating the morning quiet. Pinky threw an arm around her sister and hugged her. "I knew I could count on you, Chinks."

In the junior bunkhouse the girls rushed around finishing their cleanup chores; pre-trip excitement hung heavy in the air.

Nechama poked the broom under the last bed. "Finished! What a day to have 'sweep'! She put the broom and dustpan back on their hooks and hurried over to her cubby. She unwound the strap of her little traveling pouch and slung it over her shoulder.

"The buses are already in the parking lot," she

announced to no one in particular. She turned to Tova. "Can you look after Tzip-Tzip today?"

"Sure," said Tova. The whole bunk had grown fond of the little bird, whom they'd named "Tzip-Tzip."

"Thanks, Tova." Nechama stuffed the last essential items into her pouch and hurried out the door.

One by one, the juniors headed for the bus in the parking lot. Only two girls remained behind: Batya and Tova.

Batya sat on her bed casually sorting through her box of hair clips and waving goodbye to her friends. She wondered if her plan would work.

Tova looked at Batya, and then at her wristwatch. "You'd better hurry, or you'll miss the bus."

"I'm not going," Batya replied. "I don't skate very well, so I decided not to go." The lie stuck in her throat and she felt herself blushing. She hoped that Tova wouldn't notice.

But Tova accepted it very naturally. "Oh...I thought I was going to have the camp to myself today."

Batya wasn't sure if she should feel unwanted, but quickly decided that it was just Tova's defensive nature that made her sound that way. As a matter of fact, she thought she could detect a pleased expression in Tova's eyes.

"I'd love to really explore camp grounds," Batya said. "I've been wanting to do it all along, but the camp schedule keeps us so busy."

"Have a good time," Tova said. "Don't get lost."

Batya took a deep breath. "It's no fun exploring alone. Won't you come along?"

"Well...I've got to feed Tzip-Tzipl but I can come after that, I suppose."

Batya let out her breath. "Great! I'm going up to the kitchen to see if I can get us some sandwiches to take along. We'll have a picnic! What do you want in your sandwich?"

"Whatever they have," said Tova. "I'm not fussy."

Batya skipped happily down the tarred path. Her plan was working. She was glad that she had thought of exploring. At first she had considered a game of paddle ball, but she had quickly realized that it was out of the question for Tova. Tova never joined the other girls in athletics. Batya dreamed of the day when Tova would be confident enough to join in games and activities despite her limitations. A close friend would be a good first step in boosting Tova's ego. And now, Batya's chance was at hand.

Batya ducked to avoid a low hanging branch as she cut across the path heading for the dining room. "Oops!" she cried, narrowly avoiding a collision with Pinky, as she rounded the path from the other side.

"What are you doing here?" the two girls said simultaneously.

There was a moment of uncomfortable silence. Then Pinky laughed. "We look like two cats caught stealing the cream! I'm working on an art project, so I stayed behind." She lowered her eyes as she explained, "I'm hoping to impress Faigy with it and get to head the scenery committee for cantata."

Batya looked at her seriously. "It must be very important to you if you're willing to give up the trip."

"You're right, Batya." Pinky marveled at Batya's perceptiveness. "It is. I don't know why, but suddenly this 'one of the twins' business is getting to me. I just feel like I have to do something by myself."

Batya nodded. "I understand what you mean, I think. You don't want to be thought of as half of a person."

Pinky nodded.

"Well, you don't have to prove anything to me. Have fun." She waved and headed down the path.

Pinky waved and continued climbing the hill toward the arts and crafts closet. Good old Batya. She always understood. Suddenly, she realized that Batya hadn't explained what she was doing on camp grounds. She turned to look after her, but Batya had disappeared from sight. Now WHAT had made Batya, Bloomfield's skating champion, stay behind?

Pinky didn't have much time to wonder. She was too busy concentrating on her own project.

Since this morning's conversation with Chinky, she had been thinking hard about an idea for her project. A banner for the dining room? Some kind of activity chart?

Even now, as she made her way to the arts and crafts closet, she wasn't sure what to do that would really get Faigy's attention.

She heard the roar of the buses as they began to drive away and looked wistfully in their direction. She was glad she had decided to stay behind, and yet...she imagined the fun the girls would have, skating and eating their picnic lunches and finally returning home to camp.

Home to camp! That was it. Perfect! She had a fabulous way of catching Faigy's eye!

Pinky reached the circle of staff bungalows. She approached Mr. Grundsweig's bungalow and hesitated before knocking on the door.

Mr. Grundsweig, the camp's elderly handyman, did seem friendly, but she hadn't actually ever spoken to him, and maybe he wasn't the type one asked favors of. Pinky took a deep breath. Well, either she was going to prove herself or she wasn't. She knocked on the door.

The door flew open. "What can I do for you?" Mr. Grundsweig smiled and adjusted his cap. "I thought today was trip day."

"It was. I mean, it is." In her nervousness, Pinky tripped over her words. "I stayed behind to work on a project. I need a piece of wood to make a sign and I thought you might be able to help me."

"What size is your sign going to be?" he asked.

Pinky motioned in the air to show him what she had in mind.

"Looks like you'll be needing a pretty big board. You'll find some freshly cut leaning against the new extension to the casino. Take whatever you'd like."

"Thanks," said Pinky, hurrying out. Wow! That hadn't been bad at all.

And now for the good part. Her project....

At the other end of camp, two girls entered the shady woods together. Batya carried their picnic lunch in a canvas bag slung over her shoulder. A gentle breeze blew and the birds chirped merrily.

"It's so nice and cool in here," Batya said. "Somehow it seems as if we're miles away from camp, even though we're just a few steps away."

"Yes, that's the way I usually feel in the woods," Tova said.

"Usually? You sound experienced."

Tova smiled. "I guess you could call me experienced."

Batya waited for her to go on. Was she finally going to open up a little? But Tova remained silent.

Finally Batya spoke. "Have you spent a lot of time in the mountains?" she asked.

"I've always spent my summers in a bungalow colony with my family. It's a very woodsy area, so I got to spend a lot of time exploring and following old trails. I even had my own little hideout in the woods."

"What type of hideout?" Batya asked, genuinely interested.

"Well, there's this spot where tall, thick bushes grow. You can't see through them. But I parted them and pushed through them one day, and I discovered a small clearing in the middle. About this wide." Tova gestured with her arms to indicate a space of about six feet. "There is this big, smooth rock right in the middle of it, that makes a perfect place to sit."

"Your family didn't go there this summer?" Batya asked.

Tova's face darkened. "They did. But my mother insisted that I go to camp."

"Why?"

"She...she felt that I needed to spend time with other girls." The words came out haltingly.

"Weren't there girls in the bungalow colony?" Batya asked.

"No. It's a small place, and most of the bungalows are taken by retired couples. My uncle owns the place, so it's more affordable for my parents than a regular colony. And it's cheaper than sending me and all of my brothers off to camp."

"And you enjoyed being in such a quiet place?"

"Yes. I enjoy being by myself. The old people are really nice. I used to do things for them and...and they appreciated me. They didn't look me up and down all the time."

"The girls in camp don't look you up and down, either," Batya said softly. Tova was finally confiding in her. She just hoped she would find the right thing to say.

Tova was silent for a few moments. The girls walked around the perimeter of the camp, only a few yards into the woods. "I feel as if they do," she said finally.

"But they really don't. You just haven't given them a chance to be friendly."

Tova didn't answer. She pointed to a large, stone ledge that lay ahead. "That's a good spot for our picnic. It's almost like my hideout."

"Let's make it our hideout."

The hours flew by. The leaves rustled with delight at the little scene spread before them. The two girls, friends at last, sat side by side on the stone ledge. Before them was spread the little picnic that Batya had prepared. They laughed and chattered happily; they shared sandwiches and secrets. At last Batya began to understand Tova's sulky ways. Tova had always been shy, and when a car accident left her with a permanent limp at the age of five she had retreated into herself, avoiding friendships because she was afraid others would laugh at her, or, worse, pity her.

"Just give us a chance, Tova," Batya pleaded. "And give yourself a chance."

"Maybe I will," Tova said quietly.

Batya smiled, satisfied with the pledge. She looked at her watch and jumped up. "It's really late," she said. "The time's flown by."

"Like Tzip-Tzip," Tova laughed.

"I don't know when we'll be able to come here again," Batya said. "The camp schedule keeps us so busy, and now there's going to be cantata practice during rest hour. I wish you'd join cantata at least, so we could have a good time practicing together. Y'know — they have this background part, in which you'd only have to sway a bit to the music. I think you should try out for it."

Tova scooped up some little pebbles that lay on the ledge. One by one she flung them at the nearby trees. "I'll think about it," she said. "I really will."

With that, the two girls cleaned up the remains of their picnic and began their walk back to camp.

In the arts and crafts closet, Pinky stood back to admire her work. She had outlined the words in brown crayon. It had taken a lot of meticulous measuring with her ruler to get the dimensions correct.

Yes. It had potential to be striking.

Pinky stretched her cramped fingers. Now came the part that she loved. Painting. It always made her feel like she was bringing something to life when she finally began to brush color onto a project.

Pinky opened the paint cabinet and considered which colors to choose. For starters, the camp colors, maroon and white. And what else? She stood still for a minute, eyes roving over the shelf of paint bottles. Her glance fell upon a bottle of gold paint and her face lit up. She picked it up and examined the color more closely. "Perfect! Gold will really highlight the bridge! Let's see...black will go well with the gold, and I'll need some lively colors for the flowers, pink and purple and this bright green should be right." One by one, she placed her selection on her work table.

Pinky twisted open the bottle of black paint and dipped in a long, pointed paintbrush. Swish! Gentle strokes of black paint covered the surface of the wood. Pinky caught her breath. This was the no-return zone. Once she began to paint, the picture became permanent. She gripped the brush and leaned forward, brow furrowed in concentration.

The sun rose high in the sky and then began its daily descent. In the arts and crafts room, the paint-smudged girl worked on. Colors blended, the wood was covered, and slowly the project took shape.

Pinky glanced at the large, hand-carved, wooden clock hanging on the wall. It was getting late! Soon everyone would be back. She stood back and closed her eyes for a few seconds. Then she opened them and looked intently at her work of art. Pinky smiled. It was going to be beautiful.

Taking her paintbrush, she dabbed a little more color here, added a line there, and smoothed out the background in the center. Again and again, she stood back, paintbrush poised, and then stepped forward with some final touches. At last she was satisfied.

Circling the room, she flung all the windows open as far as she could. A warm breeze entered the room,

quickly drying the paint as Pinky hurried about
straightening up the art supplies. She recapped the
last paint bottle and put it away, then she took the
handful of brushes over to the sink and rinsed them
with some brush cleanser. Finally she scrubbed her
hands and dried them.

Pinky approached her masterpiece and touched
it gingerly with the tip of her finger. Dry. She touched
it in another few spots and confirmed it. Her project
was ready.

Pinky locked the arts and crafts room and headed
for her bunkhouse. She walked along happily, satisfied with her day's work. She could just picture the
scene. She would walk over to Faigy tonight and say,
"I have something to show you..." Wait. That really
sounded silly. And how was she going to shlep Faigy
all the way up to the arts and crafts room? Well,
maybe she could bring it to the dining room during
supper.... Pinky shook her head. She would look
ridiculous marching across the room with it. So what
could she do with it? Pinky thought it over. The best
idea, she concluded, would be to leave it in a spot
where Faigy would find it. She would go back to the
arts and crafts room right now and take her project
to Faigy's room. That would be a safe place for it.

Pinky grinned to herself. A safe place. That's
what she had told Chinky last time, during the
election campaign. And remember what had happened to those signs!

Well, I'll leave it far away from water and bubble baths, she giggled to herself.

Halfway uphill, Pinky stopped in her tracks. She clapped a hand to her forehead. Why hadn't she thought of it before? Of course. She would put it in the obvious place. Right where it belonged!

8
Homecomings

In the woods, the shadows lengthened as the hour grew late. Batya and Tova made their way back over camp grounds. Batya glanced at the empty parking lot. "They'll be back soon," she said to her friend. She could picture the noisy camp buses pulling up, full of cheering girls. Her heart gave a little twinge inside of her as she thought of all the fun that she had missed. Then she thought of the lovely afternoon she had spent. It's been worth it, she concluded. She gave a little skip as they turned up the path to their bunkhouse.

As Batya and Tova sat quietly on their beds, reading and awaiting their friends, the bus grew nearer and nearer. The warm, summer air blew through the bus's open windows, fanning the girls who sat singing and cheering together.

Raizy sat slumped in her seat, oblivious to the singing and laughing around her. She could think of only one thing. Shani, her very first real friend, was angry at her. Raizy had hoped that Shani would get over the imagined insult overnight, but today had been even worse. Shani had pointedly ignored her all day. The trip could have been a lot of fun, but not with Shani glowering at her every word. Raizy had sat glumly at the side of the rink, rolling her skate encased feet against the rink railing.

What good would it do her to be newspaper editor, if Shani was going to hold it against her? Was it worth the position if it was going to spoil her summer? If it was going to cause her to lose her very best friend?

No, it wasn't worth it.

Raizy leaned her aching head against the window. The sky was turning a hazy pink as the day drew to its end. Yellow corn fields and green rolling meadows rushed by. Here and there, red farmhouses and yellow tractors dotted the countryside. Metal mailboxes stood like sentries at the entrance to each property.

Raizy barely noticed the passing farmland. Her thoughts tossed back and forth in her mind. Finally, she came to a decision. If it had to be Shani or the newspaper, she chose Shani.

Her mind made up, Raizy tried to relax. She couldn't do anything here on the bus, with everyone sitting close by. But she would talk to Shani as soon as they got to camp.

She leaned forward, watching for the exit. The bus turned at Exit 23 and traveled along Route 7. As they approached the camp, the girls at the front of the bus began to shout and point. Raizy stood up and followed their pointing fingers. What was the commotion about?

Then she saw it. There, at the top of the hill, on the overhead arch of the camp gate, the old, shabby "Welcome to Camp Tiferes" sign had been replaced with a stunning, new one! An ornate, black gate was outlined in gold on a white background. The two support posts of the gate were intertwined with lovely flowers. The bright green of the stems and leaves and the brilliant purple and pinks contrasted beautifully against the black of the gate posts. Above the gate was a large, golden bugle and inside it, WELCOME, was spelled out in maroon lettering. Out of the bugle floated musical notes, forming the words, CAMP TIFERES. The effect was striking.

As the bus neared the camp gates the girls broke into spontaneous clapping.

"Stunning!"

"That bugle is perfect, it's so symbolic of camp!"

"Unbelievable!"

"Just what the camp needed!"

The same question was on everyone's lips. "WHO painted it?"

Raizy smiled to herself as she studied the sign. She had noticed Pinky's absence and now she recognized her friend's handiwork.

Her smile faded as the bus pulled up at the parking lot. Raizy waited impatiently for the line of girls to move forward. She saw Shani get off the bus ahead of her and start walking toward their bunkhouse. She was alone. Now was Raizy's chance to speak with her and make peace.

Raizy ran ahead and caught up with her.

"Shani, listen, I've got to talk to you."

For a minute, Raizy thought that she was just going to keep on walking. But Shani turned to her grudgingly.

"What do you want?"

"I want to talk to you — in a quiet spot. We have a few minutes until the wash-up bugle."

Shani pointed to one of the red picnic tables that dotted the front lawn. "Okay, over there."

Raizy found herself stumbling over her words. Nervously, she ran her fingertips along the cracks that lay between the planks of the tabletop. "I'll...I'll quit the newspaper. It's just not worth it to me. Your friendship means more to me than any old newspaper."

Shani looked at her, surprised and gratified. So, Raizy needed her after all. "I can't tell you what to do, Raizy. It's your decision."

"I've already decided," Raizy said. "Tomorrow, I'll

tell Chavie that I can't do it."

Shani stood up. "C'mon, Raizy, let's get going. We're going to be late for wash up." The topic seemed to be finished and done with in her mind.

Raizy stood up slowly. She had done it. But somehow, her heart didn't feel any lighter.

9

Wounded Words

Night activity was over. Chattering and laughing, girls poured through the double wooden doors of the casino and streamed along the tarred paths.

"Chinky!" At the sound of the familiar voice calling her name, Chinky turned around to see her twin running to catch up with her. Before Pinky even reached her, Chinky could guess what had happened. Pinky's flushed, excited face gave it away.

Chinky stepped onto the grassy lawn beside the path. "You got it!"

Pinky nodded vigorously as she tried to catch her breath.

"Faigy called me aside when we came into the casino. She said that she found the note that I had left on her bed, and that she was very impressed with the sign." Pinky chuckled. "She thought that the camp had had it made professionally! Then she said, 'Penina, you've proven your capabilities without a doubt. We are looking forward to having you head the scenery committee for us.' Then she asked me if I would mind missing night activity, so that we could discuss scenery plans. You can be sure I agreed! We went down to the dining room where some of the other heads were working together. We had a meeting to discuss the program so that everything would be coordinated." Pinky laughed aloud. "When Simi saw me, she said, 'Being that you did such a gorgeous job on that banner, I'll have to forgive you for not being in the drama."

Chinky smiled at her happy twin. "I'm really glad that you got it, Pinky. You worked hard for it, and it's very important to you."

Pinky was thoughtful as they walked along in the dark. "I hope you realize, Chinky, that this has nothing to do with you. I mean, I'm thrilled to be your twin, I really, really am. It's just that at the same time I feel this need to do something on my own."

"Oh, I know," said Chinky. "I didn't think of it any other way."

"Y'know," Pinky continued slowly, "I think most of all, I'm just trying to prove something to myself. It's not like I want the attention I'll get for being the head. Being in camp, among so many people who don't know me, makes me feel kind of scared and insignificant. I need to show myself that I can over-come that."

"It sounds good to me," said Chinky. "Oh, I am too tired to think through all this complicated stuff. My feet ache from all that skating — it's really been a long day."

Pinky laughed aloud as they approached their bunkhouse. "It really isn't like me to be doing all this thinking. It's more like Raizy's kind of thing. I think I'm going to concentrate on scenery now." Happily, she followed Chinky up the stairs of their bunkhouse.

The juniors milled around their bunkhouse, getting ready for bed. Nechama squeezed some mint toothpaste onto her toothbrush and gave her teeth a vigorous brushing. She rinsed her teeth and looked into the mirror. A dribble of white, foamy toothpaste had run down her chin and splattered on to her pink nightgown.

"Yick!" She carefully wiped it off with the corner of her towel and checked the mirror again. She grinned and stuck out her tongue at her image.

"NECHAMA — there's a LINE!"

"Okay, all right. I'm finished." She quickly capped her toothpaste and clicked the cover of her soap box shut. Slinging her towel over her shoulder, she clomped back to her cubby in her clogs.

Nechama sat down on her bed and rubbed her ankle. "I have a charley horse in my foot," she complained. "And I've got this terrible blister on the back of my heel. I knew I should've taken the next size skates."

She got up from the bed and sat down on the floor beside Tzip-Tzip's box. She had taken Tova's advice and had put the bird into a cardboard box with a piece of screening stretched over the open side.

"Hi, Tzip-Tzip," she said. "Were you waiting for me all day long?" The little bird fluttered its wings and hopped around the box, twittering in a happy tone.

"Do you see that?" Nechama said with pride. "She really missed me! And look how she's flapping her wing — she's really improving!"

Batya and Tova sat down on Batya's bed and peered into the cage. "You're right!" said Batya. "She really is happy to see you! She hasn't done that for us all day long."

Nechama reached into the cage and held out her finger. Tzip-Tzip hopped to a perch on her finger. "I missed you, too. You wouldn't have wanted to come on the trip though — can't picture you in roller skates!"

The girls laughed at the thought of Tzip-Tzip in roller skates. The threesome sat around the improvised bird cage, relaxed and happy. It had been a full day for everyone.

Nechama turned to Batya and Tova. "It was a fantastic trip. Pity the two of you didn't come. I missed you on the rink, Batya. I wanted to practice a couple of those tricky maneuvers, the ones that we figured out on our skates back in Bloomfield."

Batya turned red and opened her mouth in an attempt to change the subject, but Nechama continued on. "Remember that fancy figure eight pattern? The one we did in pairs? I wanted to show it to the bunk, but couldn't get it to come out right. You were always the professional between the two of us."

Tova's green eyes flashed angrily. Batya stared at her, aghast. "Tova..." she began.

Tova stood up and looked steadily at Batya's scarlet face. "So, you 'don't skate very well.' You lied to me! It was all a lie...everything you said!" Turning on her heel, she stalked out of the room.

Batya sat frozen in her place for a moment. Then she got up and ran after her.

The night was cloudy and dark. Batya rushed down the steps and stopped. Tova was nowhere in sight.

Batya walked across the lawn to the middle of the field and looked in all directions. Everything looked different in the dark. The night threw deep shadows everywhere, and the usual, peaceful scenery suddenly seemed threatening and foreboding. Even the familiar picnic table in the middle of the lawn was wrapped in mystery.

Batya shivered and wrapped her arms around her thin robe. Where could Tova have gone? Batya stood still and considered her dilemma. Any minute now, their O.D. would enter their bunkhouse, and Batya knew she would have to suffer the consequences if she wasn't there. On the other hand, if she went in now, she most probably would not get permission to leave. Batya considered waiting to talk to Tova tomorrow. No, she decided, it would have to be now, before Tova retreated into her old sullen self.

If she hadn't already.

Batya walked across the lawn, peering in all directions. "Tova, Tova!" she called. No answer. Batya circled the area, looking behind the bunkhouses for a trace of the missing girl.

The night was dark, and she completely missed the slight figure sitting in the woods right behind the junior bunkhouse. It was Tova, leaning against a large oak tree, her eyes closed and her cheeks damp and smudged. How happy she had been only a short time ago. Finally, she had felt the joy of acceptance. At last she had felt like a person, not just 'the handicapped girl.' But it had all been a lie. A scheme. She wasn't Batya's friend. She was just a charity case.

"Tova, Tova!" Tova heard Batya's repeated call. She opened her eyes and slunk back against the tree as Batya approached her hiding place.

Batya walked into the woods behind the bunkhouses. The trees creaked hauntingly as a breeze stirred their branches. Batya stopped short. She just couldn't bring herself to go in any further.

"Tova," she whispered hoarsely.

No answer.

Batya gave a quick glance toward the bunkhouse. With a start she saw the O.D. standing on the small porch, looking around. Looking, no doubt, for the two missing campers. Batya sighed wearily and turned back to face her punishment. Alone.

Fifteen minutes later, Batya lay under her covers, her teeth chattering with cold. All in all she hadn't gotten off too badly. The O.D. had given her a lecture and docked her from swimming and art tomorrow. No, the punishment didn't bother her much. What bothered her was knowing that Tova was furious with her — and not knowing where Tova was!

The sound of her bunkmate's deep breathing rose and fell around her. But Batya couldn't sleep. Not with Tova's bunk lying vacant beside her.

At last, Batya heard the sound of uneven footsteps, as someone made her way up the bunkhouse steps. The O.D. greeted Tova sharply as she entered.

"Where were you? Do you realize what time it is?"

Tova silently stared at the floor.

"What's your name?" the O.D. asked crisply.

"Tova Gutman," Tova replied sullenly.

The O.D. regarded her tear-stained countenance with concern. Her voice softened. "I'm sorry, but you are banned from swimming and art tomorrow. Now hurry into bed."

Tova got into bed without glancing in Batya's

direction. She pulled her cover up to her neck, and was silent. Batya stared miserably at her silent back.

Batya felt hot tears pricking her eyes. Everything had been going so well. And now it was all spoiled. Why had she lied to Tova? She should have known that lying would only lead to problems. She thought back over the wonderful day they had shared. Couldn't Tova see that they were truly friends anyway? But she had ruined it with her little lie...Tova ...lie...ruined...the words resounded in her mind. Batya tossed and turned and finally drifted off into a fitful sleep.

Morning dawned on Camp Tiferes. Through a cloud of sleep, Batya heard the bugle sounding. Batya groaned. Her head hurt, and her eyes felt like there was sand in them. She definitely didn't feel rested. She turned over and dug deeper under her covers, and was soon fast asleep again.

Batya awoke with a start to find Nechama shaking her shoulder. "What time is it?"

Nechama was fully dressed, siddur in hand. "It's late. Hurry up. I tried to wake you up ten times already!"

Batya jumped out of bed and looked at her watch. Nechama was right—it was really late. Everyone was dressed and ready to go daven.

Tova was nowhere in sight. Batya sighed, disappointed. She had hoped to speak to her first thing in the morning. Now it would be a while before she would be able to speak to her privately. If she would speak to her at all....

"What are you dreaming about?" Nechama asked impatiently. "If you hurry and get dressed I'll wait for you."

Batya grabbed her clothes and ran to the back of the bunkhouse. "I'll be ready in a sec," she called over her shoulder.

Batya emerged fully dressed a few minutes later. "Sorry to keep you waiting," she said as she bent to tie her shoelaces. She ran a brush through her hair, and quickly gathered it into a pony holder.

The two girls headed up the path together.

"I'm sorry about last night," Nechama said. "I didn't realize I was getting you into trouble." She looked contrite.

"Oh, it really wasn't your fault," Batya replied. "I didn't blame you at all. How could you have known that I'd said I didn't skate well?"

Nechama giggled. "It really isn't like you, to be getting into trouble, Batya. It sounds more like the kind of thing I would do."

Batya didn't laugh. "One thing I can tell you, Nechama — don't ever tell a lie." They reached the casino and quietly entered.

As soon as she finished davening, Batya looked around for Tova. But Batya had started davening late, and Tova was long finished and gone by the time she was ready to close her siddur.

Batya squeezed herself into the last space at the breakfast table. Tova was sitting at the opposite end, staring down at her food as she ate. Batya tried to catch her eye, but Tova steadily avoided her gaze. Their confrontation would have to wait for cleanup time, Batya realized.

Batya finished emptying the wastebaskets and sat down to wait for Tova to appear. Halfway through cleanup Batya realized that Tova wasn't going to appear. She checked the cleanup chart. To her chagrin, she saw that today was Tova's day to have "free." "Forget it," Batya mumbled to herself. She would never get a chance to speak to her privately during activities.

Suddenly her face brightened. They both had been docked from swimming. Now, she couldn't wait for her punishment — when she'd finally have it out with Tova.

Raizy bent over the floor of the C.I.T. bunkhouse closet, straightening out the mess. Patent leather Shabbos shoes, scuffed sneakers, and assorted slippers lay in a confused assortment at the bottom of the closet. Raizy laid them all out, side by side. She was glad that this was her cleanup chore today. It was one of the fast ones, and Raizy needed the extra time this morning.

In her mind, Raizy rehearsed the speech that she planned to make to Chavie. "I'm sorry, I won't be able to do the newspaper this summer. It just won't work out for me." The words weighed like lead on her heart. Raizy sighed. She had made a decision, and she would stick to it.

Now where was the partner to this red Dr. Scholl slipper? There it was, hidden under a sneaker. Raizy paired the last stray shoes and looked around the C.I.T. room.

Everyone was busy with cleanup chores. Shani had "sweep" this morning. She was in a great mood and swung the broom with gusto, singing under her breath as she worked. Obviously, she was satisfied with Raizy's decision. At least someone was.

Raizy stood up. She'd better rush if she was going to catch Chavie.

"Where are you off to?" Shani queried.

"I want to talk to Chavie this morning — remember?" Raizy half hoped that Shani would say something to her, show her that she could keep both her friendship and the position. But Shani just said, "Are you done with cleanup — already?"

"Yeah. I only had 'closet' today."

"Lucky you! Sweeping takes forever. I think our bunk should invest in a vacuum cleaner. What d'ya say, huh?" She whacked the broom for emphasis. "You'd better run. See you at first activity." Shani attacked the floor again, humming under her breath. Obviously sweeping didn't bother her too much.

Raizy walked slowly out of the bunkhouse. She

cut across the lawn, heading for the office. She sloshed her sneakers through the grass, wet from last night's rain.

As she approached the office, Chinky descended the office steps.

"Hi Raizy! How're you doing?" Chinky was her usual cheery self.

"Fine, I guess," Raizy answered without enthusiasm. "Is Chavie Fried in the office?"

"Chavie? Nope, I think she might be up at the casino, working with the cantata heads," Chinky replied.

"Not all the way up there!" Raizy exclaimed in dismay. "I'd better run!"

"Wait a sec. I'm going that way. Let me walk with you." Chinky caught up to Raizy and walked beside her.

The two headed uphill. Raizy trudged along with her head bent.

"What's the matter, Raizy? You look miserable." Chinky looked at Raizy searchingly.

"Oh, nothing much," Raizy mumbled.

Chinky rolled her eyes. "Don't give me that!" Then her voice softened. "Come on, we're friends, remember?"

Raizy hesitated and then blurted out, "You're right, I am miserable."

"Tell me about it," Chinky urged her.

"Choosing between two things you want very

badly can be so difficult," Raizy began slowly. Before she knew it, all her heartache came pouring out.

"So it meant choosing between Shani and the newspaper — and I...I guess I choose Shani," Raizy ended. She glanced at her watch. "Oops — I'd better run!"

Chinky caught hold of Raizy's elbow. "Wait!" she cried. "You're not going anywhere!"

Raizy stopped in surprise. "What? Why not?"

Chinky released Raizy's elbow. "Listen, this is not your problem — it's Shani's. You're not doing anything wrong by accepting editorship. It's Shani who has to learn how to handle it!"

Raizy shook her head wearily. "I can't, Chinky. It's just not worth making my whole summer miserable. I'd —"

"No. You're wrong." Chinky shook her head emphatically. "Do you remember the time that you quit the *B.Y. Times*, way back at the first issue? Now that was a matter of principle. You wouldn't have anything to do with a newspaper that went against halachah. But this isn't principle at all. It's...it's just cowardice! You've got to be strong about what's right. I'm sure Shani will eventually come around."

Raizy sat down on a big rock that lay alongside the path. She cupped her chin in her hands, brow wrinkled in thought. "I guess...I guess you're right," she said slowly. "But this is not going to be easy."

"If you do what's right, everything will work out

in the end," Chinky said.

"It's easy for you to say," Raizy sounded dejected.

"I do have some experience with this," Chinky countered. "Pinky and I were approached by Simi, the dramatics head at cantata tryouts. She wanted us to do a cutesy twin act. Pinky and I had other plans, of course."

"So what did you do?"

"We just didn't give in. We had to do what was right for us."

"I guess that wasn't easy, either."

"No, it wasn't. As a matter of fact, we risked losing a chance to be in cantata altogether. Simi is a staff member, and her word carries weight with Faigy."

"So what happened?"

"Well, Pinky is getting to head scenery, for one thing. She stuck to her principles and it worked. You'll be doing what's right, Raizy." Chinky repeated. "That's what counts."

Raizy stood up. "Thanks, Chinky. Thanks a lot. I guess I'd better get back to my bunk now." She hesitated for a moment and then turned and walked slowly back toward her bunk.

10
It's Only Fair

Raizy entered the C.I.T. bunkhouse. It was completely deserted. She looked at her watch in surprise. It was already five minutes into first activity! She had been so absorbed in conversation with Chinky, that she hadn't even heard the bugle sounding.

Their first activity this morning was swimming. Raizy was already wearing her bathing suit under her clothes, so she just slipped into her terry robe and bathing slippers.

Raizy hurried uphill toward the swimming pool. Instruction was usually first and she was already late. She hoped their instructor would excuse her.

What would she say to Shani? Different approaches ran through her head. Raizy sighed. Somehow, Shani just didn't seem to see things from her point of view. And Raizy knew she had complicated matters further by offering to give up the position. Now how would Shani react to this turnabout?

Raizy stepped off the path and walked alongside it. She loved the feeling of the green grass tickling her toes through her open slippers. The sounds of laughter, shouting, and water splashing greeted her from afar. It sounded like everyone was having a grand time.

The swimming instructor frowned as Raizy joined her group.

"I'm sorry," Raizy apologized. "I had something important to take care of."

Shani caught her eye and winked. Raizy avoided her gaze.

"That's no excuse for coming late. Next time you are to report to the pool area first, and then receive permission to leave."

"Okay. Sorry," Raizy said meekly. Nothing seemed to be going her way today.

"That's it for today," continued the instructor. "You have free swim now. Practice the crawl as you swim. Enjoy!"

The bunk dispersed in different directions, most of the girls heading for the water.

"Hi," said Shani cheerily. "What did she say?"

"Let's go sit on the bleachers in the sun," Raizy suggested. "It's too chilly to go right into the water."

The two girls headed for the metal bleachers at

the back of the pool area. Raizy climbed up a couple of rows and sat down. The sun-warmed metal felt good to the touch, and Raizy leaned against it.

Shani sat down hugging her pink terry robe around her. "It's pretty cool today. The water must be freezing after last night's rain. Now tell me, what happened with Chavie?"

"Well it's like this," Raizy began. "I was going to talk to her, but —"

"You mean you didn't speak to her?" Shani asked her. She sat up straight on the bench, her eyebrows raised in suspicion.

"Well, while I was looking for her," Raizy began, "I realized that we were making a mistake..."

"A mistake? Why's that?" Shani's voice rose shrilly.

"Because...because the newspaper has nothing to do with our friendship." Raizy groped for the right words. "Chavie just happened to pick me to be editor. It had nothing to do with you. I certainly didn't mean to insult you in any way, so..."

Shani stood up and scrambled down from the bleachers. "So, nothing!" she called over her shoulder.

"Wait, one minute, let me finish what I was saying," Raizy called urgently, climbing down after her.

Shani turned around and planted her hands on her hips. "Are you going to talk to her, or aren't you?"

"I'm not, but..." Raizy didn't get to finish her sentence.

Shani's eyes flashed angrily. "I can't be friends with someone who changes her mind every minute. Forget it!"

Raizy watched sadly as Shani walked off in a huff toward the pool. She hoped she was doing the right thing. One thing was certain, though. It wasn't easy.

The juniors headed for their bunkhouse to change into swimsuits and robes. Nechama caught up to Batya and walked alongside her. "Come on, I'll race you to the bunkhouse. I want to get to the pool early today."

"I'm in no rush," Batya said. "No swimming for me today, remember?"

"Forgot. Too bad." Nechama sympathized. "You picked the right day. The water is probably cold after last night. It was a real country storm."

"Uh huh," Batya murmured. She was only half-listening, as she planned out her confrontation with Tova.

The juniors were soon ready, and one by one left for the pool. Tova was busy at her cubby, Batya observed. Suddenly she noticed Batya sitting on her bed. Hastily she grabbed something from her cubby and headed for the door.

"Wait!" cried Batya, springing up from the bed. Tova continued on out the door. Batya ran after her. "Please, Tova, won't you at least let me explain?"

Tova half-turned, one hand still clutching the

porch railing. "What do you want from me? You're not my friend. It was all a lie! Everything was a lie!"

Batya looked at her pleadingly. "I really meant it. I didn't want to go skating. I wanted to stay on campgrounds with you. I just —"

"You lied to me," Tova repeated bitterly. "It was all a fake."

Batya took a deep breath. "I did lie. I'm sorry — it wasn't the right thing to do. But our friendship IS real. I wanted to spend the day with you, and I couldn't think of a different excuse. I should have told you the truth. But I didn't think you'd believe me. I was wrong, and I'm sorry."

Tova stared at her without hearing what she was saying. "It wasn't real," she said stonily. "You just care for me the way Nechama cares for her wounded bird. You just want something to pity. Well, look for someone else!" Tova stomped to the steps and started walking down.

Batya felt frustrated and hurt. She couldn't help herself; the words, angry and bitter, came pouring out. "It's you who are full of pity — for yourself! Can't you see that? Or does your self-pity blind you to everything?"

Silence was the only reply.

The day grew warmer. The first cantata rehearsal had been called for rest hour. From all over the camp, girls swarmed to the casino.

Simi, head of dramatics in Camp Tiferes, stood upon the stage to address the girls.

Simi banged on a lectern and the room grew quiet. The girls listened attentivly as Simi spoke.

"The cantata will take place at the end of first trip, which coincides with the beginning of the Three Weeks. Our timely theme will be '*Am Yisrael Netzach*.' Despite all the persecution that we have suffered at the hands of other nations, *Am Yisrael* survives and even flourishes. The different acts of the cantata will represent the different exiles and the destruction of the *Beis HaMikdash*. Our drama group will narrate the presentation and will tie the whole theme together. They will also put on a couple of skits that tie into our theme. There will be a short skit on the Greek era, and also a skit on the Holocaust.

"Our choir group will sing songs representative of the different times. We have beautiful medleys planned for each act. Our dance group will also be representing the different times; we have a market dance scene from the time of the Romans, for example.

"Our last act will concentrate on the time of *Mashiach*, when the *Beis HaMikdash* will be rebuilt of fire itself, and will be indestructible.

"That is our theme," she concluded. "There is potential for this cantata to be an inspiring, beautiful performance. However, we need your complete cooperation. Rehearsals must begin on time and proceed in an orderly fashion."

Simi looked seriously at the quiet, excited faces before her. She was silent for a moment, and then she spoke. This time her tone was crisp and business-like.

"You have all already seen your names posted on the bulletin board, and are aware of which groups you are in. I would like to announce the head of our scenery team — Penina Chinn. We are fortunate in having Pinky with us this summer. The work she has shown us is proof of her exceptional talents in this field. Pinky, under your direction, I'm sure your team will produce magnificent work."

Pinky blushed and sat up straight. The theme outline had already created visions in her mind. Nothing definite yet, but lots of ideas to work with.

"We are ready to begin," Simi continued. "Please join your groups. Drama will meet onstage, dance will meet at the handball court. Choir will meet at the bleachers and the costume and scenery commit-tees will meet in the casino." Simi gave everyone a broad smile. "And good luck to us all!"

The crowd broke up, each group heading for its meeting place. Shani and Chinky joined the drama group onstage. The girls looked around rather ner-vously. Though their names had appeared on the list of girls chosen for parts in the cantata, no one knew what part she'd been cast for.

The girls sat around on the stage floor, waiting for Simi to join them.

"You know something?" Shani remarked. "This is a great spot. It's real cozy with the curtains shut."

"We could have a drama club meeting here regularly," said Chinky. "We could act out different scripts and have a lot of fun."

"It's a good idea," Rina said. "But between the cantata, the major play, and the song and dance festival, the stage is occupied just about the whole summer. Anyway, if you get accepted into the other productions too, you'll be practicing the whole summer in any case."

"Do you know which play they are putting on this year?" Shani inquired. "That's what I'd really like to be in."

"No idea," Rina answered. "But you can ask Simi."

"Ask me what?" Simi parted the curtains and stepped onto the stage.

"We were wondering which play will be performed this year."

"That's top secret," Simi laughed. "Sorry, you'll know in good time! We'd better get on with this cantata rehearsal now. Never mind the major play."

Simi sat down on a chair and smoothed out the pile of scripts on her lap. "Okay, we don't have much time today, so we are going to do as follows. You'll each receive a script. Your part is written on top of the page. Then I'll read through the script so that you can get familiar with it."

The girls sat quietly, anxious and tense, as Simi

called their names, one by one. "Shani Baum," she said. Shani walked quickly to the front of the stage, anticipation in her step. She accepted the script and returned to her seat without looking at it. She sat down and slowly unfolded the page. "Shani Baum — Musician," was written in red. Shani smiled, satisfied. The Musician was a good part. She glanced at Chinky, who'd just received her script from Simi. Chinky looked happy. She must have gotten a good part, too. Shani was happy for her friend. She had been afraid that Chinky would feel put down with all the attention that Pinky was getting.

The girls sat around the stage and focused on Simi, who began to read. "It happened long ago, in the days of..." Simi's voice changed with each part that she read. Her melodious voice accented the subtle messages of each word. The play came alive for the girls, as each listened attentively to how each part should be read.

Abruptly, Simi's reading came to an end. "That's it for now, girls." Simi stuck her script into her clipboard. "The bugle will be sounding in just a few minutes. We'll finish the script next time. In the meantime, practice saying your parts, and start learning them by heart."

The girls filed out of the casino. Shani hummed as she strolled along the path with Chinky. "I got the part of the musician. I think I'll enjoy it. Which part did you get?"

"I'm going to be the woman from the inn," Chinky answered.

Shani stopped in surprise. "But that's not even a speaking part!"

Chinky smiled. "It's just one line of speaking and a lot of hanging around the stage."

Shani shook her head. "That's not fair. Such a tiny part? How could they do that to you? Especially with all the attention that Pinky will be getting!"

"It is fair," Chinky answered. "After all, I'm me and Pinky is Pinky. Different people with different talents. That's what we're always trying to tell people, right?"

Shani looked at Chinky, astonished. Her friend didn't seem disturbed in the least.

"But you can act! They could have given you a bigger part!" Shani declared. The slight to her friend rankled.

"Look," Chinky said slowly, "they only have a certain amount of big parts to give out. Maybe in the major play something better will work out for me. And if not..." Chinky shrugged.

Shani couldn't understand Chinky's calm acceptance of the situation. "Well, it seems to me that it wasn't fair to divide things so unevenly between you and Pinky," she declared.

"Sometimes my talents are needed, and sometimes Pinky's are," Chinky responded. "I got loads of attention this year. Don't forget, just last month, I ran for president — and won. It's Pinky's turn now. That's all. I'm happy for her. I'd be a pretty rotten sister, and a pretty rotten friend, if I let her success bother me."

"I guess so," Shani said slowly. Somehow this whole thing sounded familiar. As if it applied to her.

The trumpeting sound of the bugle swept over the camp. "I'm going to run," Chinky said cheerily. "We have swimming now and I still have to change. Bye!" She took off down the path, sneakers skipping across the pavement.

Shani walked slowly along the path, pausing to send little pebbles rolling with a kick of her foot. Chinky's words echoed in her brain. "Different people have different talents," Shani mused. And different moments to enjoy the limelight.

Raizy is the writer — and it's her turn now.

"...a pretty rotten friend, if I let her success bother me." What kind of friend had she been?

What kind of friend would she turn out to be?

For a moment Shani felt completely downcast. Well, it wasn't fair! The whole newspaper had been her idea. Then she kicked herself mentally. What a fool she was being! She had her own attributes and talents to be thankful for. She could give herself credit for organizing their school newspaper and bringing Raizy's talent to light. There was nothing demeaning about Raizy's being chosen, and no earthly reason why she shouldn't accept Raizy's offer to work with her. Raizy had never meant to insult her — and she'd been a fool to feel insulted!

Shani wasn't one to stay down for long. She stared ahead determinedly. She was going to accept the offer of assistant to Raizy, and she would do it happily. Shani brightened — assistant editor wouldn't be so bad after all. Maybe she could do an article based on the cantata....

But plans had to wait. First, there was important business to take care of. Shani knew what had to be done to take away the sour feeling that had collected over this whole business. She glanced at her wristwatch and hurried along the path.

The C.I.T. bunk was milling around the handball court. Off to one side sat a slightly stooped figure. Raizy.

She was sitting by herself, head cupped in her palms, too miserable to join in the game. She saw Shani hurrying up the path and gave a deep sigh. The silent treatment was about to begin once again.

Shani could see her bunk as she approached. Where was Raizy? Shani breathed in relief. Perfect! She was sitting alone and they would be able to talk. Poor kid! She looked miserable.

Shani broke into a run.

11
Soaring Free

"*Yibaneh, yibaneh, yibaneh hamikdash....*" The dining room rocked with the sound of the campers' voices lifted in song. Batya joined the others in enthusiastic harmony.

"*Yibaneh, yibaneh....*" The singing continued, enthusiastic as before, but Batya suddenly grew silent. She thought about the *Beis HaMikdash* and remembered that morning's *shiur*.

Their *shiur* counselor had spoken about *sinas chinam*, hatred of other Jews, and how it had been the cause of the *Beis HaMikdash*'s destruction. She had developed her idea beautifully, with many stories and parables. She had ended the discussion with an interesting thought.

"Girls," she had said, "I just want to end today's *shiur* with a parable that I'm sure you already know.

Think of a bundle of twigs. If we were to try to snap the bundle in half, we would find it very difficult to do so. However, were we to take each twig individually, we would easily be able to break them.

"The strong bundle of twigs is compared to *Klal Yisrael* at the time when there is peace and unity between all Jews. The weak, little twigs represent the Jews when they are divided by *sinas chinam*.

"Let's just think for a moment about those weak, little twigs. Suppose we have a bunk of girls who are all friends, except for one girl who has not been befriended by the bunk. Who does the weak, little twig represent?

"Simple — so you might think. The one girl standing alone is the weak, little twig. But you know what, girls? You'd be wrong. The entire bunk — not just the one friendless girl — has become a bunch of weak, little twigs.

"Girls, none of us is perfect. When we are judged as a whole, your friends' merits make up for your deficits. But when we are divided, Hashem has to judge us individually, and then we are sadly lacking.

"We must have *achdus*! If not, it is we who have become the weak, little twigs."

And here I sit, thought Batya, singing *"Yibaneh,"* while Tova sits at the other end of the table and won't even glance in my direction. This is the *achdus* that I've brought to my bunk.

Batya sighed. She had tried to speak to Tova this

morning, but it was like talking to a stone wall. She only wished that she hadn't lost her temper and accused Tova of self-pity. She knew she had only added insult to injury.

Words, words, words. They slip so easily out of our mouths and can never be recalled. Like that little lie that she had told. Batya sighed again.

The song ended and the usual chatter filled the dining room. After a few minutes, head counselor Chavie Fried held up her hands for silence. The room was instantly quiet.

"Good afternoon, Camp Tiferes. We sound so beautiful today! Now for a couple of announcements. *Ohel Aleph* can proceed to the canteen during rest hour to receive their reward for winning cleanup. *Ohel Aleph*, keep up the good work! All shoes that are in need of repair should be given into the office during rest hour. There is no cantata practice today. Please take this opportunity to write letters. Remember, your families are waiting to hear from you."

"C.I.T.s dismissed!"

"Seniors dismissed!"

"Juniors dismissed!"

Batya and Nechama left the dining room together. "What's all that food you're carrying, Nechama?" Batya asked curiously, gazing at the bag of canteen nosh that Nechama was holding.

"Goodbye party," Nechama said glumly.

"Goodbye party? For who?" Batya looked anxious.

Could it be that Tova was leaving?

"For Tzip-Tzip. She's really flying around her cage. I don't think it would be fair to keep her cooped up any longer," Nechama said, with a wistful little sigh.

"Oh, for Tzip-Tzip," Batya said, relief tinging her voice. "I'm glad there's no cantata practice today. I wouldn't want to miss this."

They entered the bunkhouse together. Nechama rushed over to the cage.

"Come on, everybody," Batya called. "We're having a goodbye party for Tzip-Tzip!"

The Juniors gathered around Nechama.

"Are you really setting her free, today?"

"We're going to miss her!"

The girls sat around the cage on the surrounding beds. Nechama handed out wafers and passed around a bag of cookies.

"What should we sing?" they joked. " 'We Hate to See You Go' or '*Ki Vesimchah Teitzeiyu*'?"

"How about 'The Little Bird Is Calling'?" somebody suggested.

But Nechama was serious as she fed the bird her last meal of cracker crumbs. And the other girls, following her example, stopped joking around and began to sing.

When all the food was gone and everyone had quieted down, Nechama stood up. "Well," she said, "I guess it's time."

Nechama went outside and walked toward the edge of the playing field where she had found Tzip-Tzip, the bird's box held carefully in both her hands. The bunk followed behind. The girls sensed that this was serious business for their usually jolly friend, and no one said a word.

Nechama placed the cage on the grassy ground. "Are you ready, Tzip-Tzip?" she asked. "Remember — you can always come visit."

She opened the cage door and put in her hand. Tzip-Tzip flew to perch on her finger. Nechama withdrew her hand from the cage and held it aloft. The little bird sat tight. A little breeze ruffled its feathers.

"Fly away, Tzip-Tzip!" Nechama called. The little bird cocked its head and looked at Nechama. Then, with a soft rustle it spread its wings and flew off. It landed on the grass a few yards away. For a few seconds it hopped around on the grass, looking back at the girls. Finally, it took off. Its wings flapped gracefully as it flew higher and higher.

"Good luck, Tzip-Tzip. Goodbye!" the girls cried.

"Goodbye! Farewell, Tzip-Tzip!" Nechama called. She watched the little bird as it soared upward, her face glowing, her eyes both happy and sad.

Batya touched Nechama on the arm. "You'll have time to get back into camp life now. You've been so busy with Tzip-Tzip that you've hardly been involved in sports or anything."

"Yeah," said Nechama. Her eyes still followed the

faraway speck.

"You really were a good mother to that bird, poor thing." Batya regarded her old friend with newly found respect. It was funny how this bird episode had really changed Nechama. Batya remembered the time Nechama had tried to change herself by becoming overly studious and serious during the school year. It had only been a cosmetic change, and it didn't take long for everyone to see that she was still the same Nechama — impetuous, fun-loving, sometimes irresponsible. But this was different. This time Nechama had changed gradually. Nursing the little bird back to health had awakened a new, serious, gentle part in Nechama's personality. It complemented her and seemed to be here to stay.

Nechama looked seriously at her friend. "I didn't care for it out of pity," she said. "I loved that bird. I really did."

Tova looked up. She had been standing off to one side of Nechama, and couldn't help overhearing the conversation. Pity, love — the two words repeated themselves in her mind. The two are sometimes difficult to tell apart, she thought confusedly.

The bunk drifted back toward the bunkhouse, Nechama at the center. Tova lagged behind. She wasn't in the mood for the noisy bunkhouse. She needed some thinking time. Where could she go? Suddenly it hit her. Their hideout. The perfect spot.

Tova headed up the path as quickly as her feet

could carry her. By the time she reached the woods behind the casino, she was out of breath. This was the spot that they had emerged from on that day. Would she be able to find the hideout now?

She stepped into the shade of the woods. The bushes that had concealed their hideout lay directly ahead — at least she thought they were the bushes. She parted the bushes, and breathed a sigh of relief. There was the stone ledge — she had found the hideout.

Tova climbed onto the rock and drew her knees up. She wrapped her arms around them and began to relax. It was so peaceful here. The trees arched overhead, bits and pieces of bright blue sky peeping through their leafy glory. Around her, the different shades of green and brown outlined in the oddly shaped trees and bushes were woven together to form a soft wonderland. The woods were quiet, the silence broken only by the soft whispering of the leaves and the twittering birds.

Pity and love — they were sometimes hard to tell apart. "I didn't care for it out of pity. I loved that little bird," Nechama had said. True, Nechama really had found it hard to part from Tzip-Tzip. She had enjoyed caring for it and seeing it heal. Nechama had given so much of herself for the bird that she had come to love it.

Nechama had taken the bird out of pity. Tova frowned. She detested being pitied. Had Batya become her friend out of pity, too? Was she just an object of pity?

Tova shook her head, confused. She looked around as if searching for an answer in the woods. Memories of their day spent together in this hideout came flooding back. They had certainly enjoyed each other's company. How good it had felt to laugh together and talk! Tova shook her head with certainty. Batya could not be that good of an actress. They definitely had been true friends.

And even before that day — hadn't Batya kept on pushing her to participate in more activities and to try out for cantata? That certainly wasn't pity. Sometimes, she didn't even seem to sympathize!

Batya had accused her of self-pity. That hurt. Tova forced herself to consider it. Perhaps it was true. Was she creating her own misery? Perhaps Batya liked her, and only felt sorry that she pitied herself.

Tova rubbed her aching head. All this soul-searching was painful. One thing seemed clear. She would be a fool to give up the friendship. Whatever had started it, it was a real friendship now.

From afar, Tova heard the bugle calling. Rest hour was over. It was time to face the world. She knew what she had to do next. Apologize. It takes strength to apologize, she realized. She was used to people apologizing to her, and it would take courage to be the one to do it this time.

Tova took a deep breath as she stood up and pushed aside the bushes. It was time to gather her courage.

Shani looked around her at the beautifully landscaped garden nearby. "This sure beats the *B.Y. Times* staff room at school, Raizy," she grinned.

Raizy gave her an answering smile. "Nothing beats that little room, Shani," she said. "You know that as well as I do."

"Well, maybe you're right. We had a lot of good times there — that's for sure!"

Raizy nodded. "And now, to work," she said, picking up a pad and pencil. "We can have a summary of the cantata theme written up for the editorial," she said.

"Uh huh," Shani nodded. "And we'll do an interview with Simi. That is, if the editor agrees," she corrected herself hastily.

Raizy giggled. "You're really funny, Shani. It's a good idea. Of course I agree!"

"We'll need some articles on different camp themes," Shani remarked.

"For instance?" Raizy asked.

"Um," said Shani, her cheeks blushing a fiery red. "For instance, friendship and *achdus*." They laughed together.

The two bent over their notepads scribbling and chatting. Raizy sighed with pleasure. Just like old times, she thought.

"Hi, you two," Rina cut across the green lawn toward them. "What are you up to?" she asked.

"Staff meeting," Shani said. "We're planning out the camp newspaper. I'm Raizy's assistant."

"Take a seat and join us," invited Raizy.

Rina slid onto the red wooden bench. "What type of articles are you going to put in it?"

"We're just discussing that," said Shani. "The newspaper is supposed to summarize the first trip of camp. So we want to cover all the major events and themes."

"You mean like a write-up on the trip, cantata, and color war?" Rina asked.

"Yes. Plus articles on different camp themes — like friendship and *achdus*." Raizy continued scribbling as she spoke.

"Nature!" Shani exclaimed. "We have to do something on that topic. We're just about surrounded by it here in camp!"

"You could write something on stars, Raizy," Rina added. "Hey, you know something? We've never been back to the casino field to do some more stargazing."

"Stars? Casino field?" Shani looked puzzled. "Oh, is that what you were doing out there the other night?"

"Well," said Raizy, "I left the casino that night because I had a headache." She looked straight at Shani as she spoke. "Rina came looking for me, and we got carried away by the stars. They're really clear and sharp out there."

"It's a pity we missed out on the game, though," Rina said. "I heard you were great. I didn't realize how much time had passed until we saw everyone leaving the casino."

"Let's go out there again tonight," said Raizy. "It's really so gorgeous."

"I'd love to," Shani said. So that's what they'd been doing! She'd been so sure they were discussing the newspaper and her refusal. Good old Raizy! She should've known that Raizy would stick to her principles. She kicked herself for not judging her friend favorably. What a lot of aggravation she could have saved herself from! Relief flooded her being, as the last of the sour feelings evaporated into thin air.

"Okay," Rina said. "If we meet there immediately after night activity is over, we can have fifteen minutes before we have to be in the bunkhouse."

"It's a deal," Shani said. Her slightly lopsided grin lit up her face.

"Great!" Raizy smiled contentedly. They were a threesome at last!

Tova walked slowly along the path toward the junior bunkhouse. The camp had just finished lunch and everyone was returning to their bunks for rest hour. Since her stay in the woods yesterday, she had been trying to summon the courage to actually apologize to Batya. But somehow every time she finally had a chance to speak to her alone the words had just stuck in her throat.

Tova took a deep breath. Maybe she should just leave things as they were. It would be so much easier to just keep up the silence barrier. She could just sit down on her bed and retreat once more into her private world.

Tova dragged her feet up the bunkhouse steps. Someone was sitting on the porch. It was Batya. Tova paused and then squared her shoulders.

"Hi, Batya." Tova squirmed uncomfortably.

"Oh, Tova. Hello." Batya sounded surprised.

"I, um, can I speak to you for a few minutes...."

"Sure." Batya looked at her questioningly.

"I've been doing some thinking," Tova said slowly. "I'm sorry that I said our friendship isn't real — I shouldn't have said it."

"I'm sorry, too!" Batya couldn't believe her ears. Was Tova actually willing to be her friend? "I shouldn't have lied, no matter what. It was the wrong thing to do. I guess it just seemed like the easy way out at the time. I really wanted to be able to stay behind that day, so that I'd have a chance to get to know you."

Tova was silent. She thought about what Batya was saying.

"It was nothing like Nechama with her bird," Batya added. "I'm not interested in you as...as a wounded bird. I would just like to be your friend."

The words were music to Tova's ears. She simply smiled. "So would I."

There was an awkward silence. Then Tova glanced at her watch. "Isn't it time for cantata rehearsal?"

Batya jumped up. "That's right! I'd better run! See you later, Tova." Batya hurried down the porch steps.

"Hey, what's your rush? Wait for me!" Tova descended the porch steps as fast as she could manage.

Batya turned around in surprise. "Where are you going?"

"To cantata rehearsal, of course," Tova laughed shyly. "I tried out for that background part, this morning — and I got it!"

Batya stared at her in shock and delight. "Great!" she exclaimed. "Come on, let's go."

Together they walked up the path toward the casino. Batya inhaled deeply. The smell of green grass, flowers, and trees basking in the sun, filled her lungs. She sighed happily.

"You know what, Tova?" she said to her friend as they walked together. "It's gonna be one great summer."

Camp Chronicles

A SUMMER IN TIFERES
By Raizy Segal

Summertime in camp. It's a time to relax. It's a time to have fun. It's a time for unstructured learning. It's a time for activity and creativity. It's a time of sunshine and greenery. It's a time for new and old friendships. And it's a time for growing.

A month of this wonderful time has already passed. What an experience it has been! The hills and mountains have echoed with our laughter, and the trees and stones have witnessed our fun as we have participated in day after day of fun-filled activity: energy-charged ball games, stunning arts and crafts, splashing in the swimming pool, and fantastic night events. Trip day, hiking, field trip, and cantata practice all have added to the excitement. And stimulating *shiurim* have kept us on the Torah path.

Old friendships have been renewed, and many new friendships have been formed. Talents, new and old, have been put to the test. Friendships have brought out the best in us. New experiences have challenged us. It has been a time of growth for all of us.

INTERVIEW

Interview with Simi Leifer, dramatics head for cantata.

By Shani Baum

S.B. What will the cantata theme be this year?

S.L. The theme of the cantata will be "The Eternal Jew." We will be presenting the theme in song, drama, and dance. We will travel through the different exiles that our nation has suffered through.

S.B. What do you mean by "The Eternal Jew"?

S.L. We will be concentrating on the fact that our nation has always survived and will always survive, despite persecution, because the Jewish people is eternal.

S.B. What else can you tell me about the cantata?

S.L. Well, there's the final act, which centers on the time of *Mashiach*. All in all, it should be a very inspiring performance, not to be missed.

S.B. When will it take place?

S.L. At the end of first trip — the night before the banquet.

S.B. Thanks for all the information. We wish you lots of luck and I'm sure it will be fantastic!

STARS
By Raizy Segal

I'm sitting in the grass one night in the country with some friends. We talk and we argue, all involved in the little details of our lives. We are so important, so knowing. I give my opinion, I'm so sure I'm right. I know what I know. As someone else continues the conversation, I chance to look upward. The sky is black, broken by the scattered stars forming their age-old patterns. They are so far, far away. So much is between us. I feel like I am shrinking inside myself until I am just a little dot. The stars are all staring down at me and some seem to laugh at me. How wise they are! Night after night, age after age, they are at their posts — watching, listening. Processions of people pass before them — going through the phases of life. People are born, they struggle with life, some fail, some succeed, and then they're gone. We're so involved in ourselves, we have such belief in our control of our little worlds. How those little stars must laugh at our self-importance. They know we're just passing through like the generations upon generations before us. I feel so small and insecure now. Who am I — and what do I know? I look upward again and some still seem to laugh, but there are those that twinkle

3

encouragingly. So whenever I get all wrapped up in nonsense, I look upward for that reminder of the eternal.

TRIP DAY!
By Esti Landau, *Ohel* 't

What a great time we had! At nine o'clock in the morning, the buses were rolling out of the parking lot. We cheered and sang our heads off all the way down Route 7. The passing scenery was a perfect backdrop for our singing.

When we reached Mountainville Skating Rink, we all lined up to be fitted for skates. The rink managers played our favorite camp tape. Then the fun started.

At first it was difficult for me to skate because I haven't skated all year. I kept on tripping over my own feet like a big klutz. I hugged the wall railing and kept hoping I wouldn't land on my head.

Then slowly I found myself gliding along, cautiously at first and then faster and faster. Skate, skate, skate, and glide! Elation filled me. I circled the rink, feeling as if I'd sprouted wings. Becoming more adventurous, I joined some of the games being played in the middle. We had to pass under a stick which was being lowered each time. I sailed boldly across the rink when it was my turn, but when I bent down to go under the stick, I fell right over. That punched a good hole in my ego!

I was aching all over by the time the day was through, but all in all, we really had a great time.

FAREWELL TO TZIP-TZIP
By Shuli Rubinfeld, Junior

The juniors had a surprise addition to their bunk this summer. It wasn't a girl, or even a person. Can you guess? I'll give you a hint. It had wings and it chirped. You got it. It was a bird.

While chasing after a ball during an activity one afternoon, Nechama Orenstein stumbled upon a wounded bird. She brought it to our bunkhouse and put it in a box so that its wounded wing would heal.

The little bird chirped at us from its perch and transformed our bunkhouse into a real cozy nest. We all grew fond of her, and one day we decided to name her. After much deliberation we decided on the name Tzip-Tzip. Nechama cared for her devotedly and fed her three times a day. We all enjoyed watching her wing get better from day to day.

After a few days, Tzip-Tzip started to flutter her wounded wing, and Tova Gutman came up with the idea of covering her box with screening. Soon she was really flying around in the cage.

With sadness in our hearts, we gathered around one rest hour for a goodbye party. Then Nechama took Tzip-Tzip to the edge of the woods and released her. The little bird kept looking back at us as if she, too, would miss us. Then she stretched her wings and flew off.

Our bunkhouse felt empty for a while. We miss her merry chirp, but we are all happy that her wing has healed and she is able to fly again.

5

IN THE WAYS OF OUR FATHERS
By Breiny Silver, *Ohel* 'ד

In *perek* 'א, mishnah 'ד, it says, *"Get yourself a friend and judge each person favorably."*

The question is asked, what is the connection between them?

The answer is that if a person does not judge his friend favorably, this will result in his losing his friendship. The only way to maintain a healthy friendship is by remembering that things aren't always as they seem. Give your friend the benefit of the doubt and you will be the winner.

Goldie and Chanie were seventh-graders who had been best friends since second grade. Chanie was a math whiz, while Goldie found math very difficult. The class had an important math test scheduled for Tuesday. On Monday afternoon Goldie got nervous. How would she ever pass? She asked Chanie to please study with her that day. Chanie apologized, explaining that although she would love to study with Goldie, she had to go right home to help her mother.

After finishing the math test the next day, Esti turned around to Goldie with a happy smile. "I'm so excited," she said. "I knew the answers, for a change. It must be because Chanie studied with me."

Goldie's heart sank. Not only had she probably failed the test, she had been betrayed by her best friend. Chanie had studied with

6

Esti! Goldie ignored Chanie for the remainder of the day.

Thinking it over that night, Goldie decided to call Chanie and at least give her a chance to explain herself. Chanie sounded puzzled when she heard Goldie's voice.

"Why were you ignoring me the whole day?" she asked.

"I was very upset when Esti told me that you had studied with her for the test. I thought you said your mother needed your help, and that is why you couldn't study with me." The hurt was obvious in Goldie's voice.

"I did. But I studied with her last Sunday," Chanie answered. There was a moment of silence, then they both laughed together. A friendship had been saved.

ALMA MATER — TIFERES — SUMMER 1992
Composed by the C.I.T.s

High up in the mountains,
Circled by green hills,
Lies our favorite camp,
It's Tiferes by name
And throughout the world has fame
As the best place in the mountains.
Tiferes, our home away from home,
Your fields and paths we love to roam,
Your *ruach* and spirit fill the air
And bring us back year after year.
Never a day without excitement,
Never a girl without a friend,
Tiferes, we yearn ten months for you,
We will remain forever true!

THANK YOU TO HENDY SHORT FOR TYPING UP THE
NEWSPAPER!

TIFERES STARS

CLEANUP – *OHEL* 'ג!!
SHIUR CONTEST – *OHEL* 'ו!!
SINGING CONTEST – *OHEL* 'ט!!
ATHLETES OF THE TRIP – CHINKY CHINN, SENIOR
RACHEL SCHREIBER, CHAVIE SURE – JUNIORS
BUNK OF THE TRIP – *OHEL* 'ד!!
CONGRATULATIONS TO ALL OF OUR SHINING
STARS!!

13
Mail Call

inky bounced into the bunkhouse, skipped to her cubby, grabbed a pen and paper, and leaped onto her bed. Her cheeks were flushed, her eyes were glowing.

"What're you up to now, Pinky?" her counselor, Suri Solomon, called up to her. "Have you finished telling every single camper your news?"

Pinky laughed. "I suppose everyone here in Tiferes knows, Suri. That's why I'm branching out to other camps in the mountains!" She waved her lavender, flowered stationery back and forth.

"Well, have fun writing," Suri said. "But tell me, Pinky, when are you coming back down to earth?"

Pinky carefully uncapped her pen and put a large book on her bed to serve as a desk. "Me? Come back down to earth?" she said merrily. "Never!"

With that, she turned her attention to the blank page in front of her.

Chani Kaufman
Bunk 12A
Camp Shalva
Woodburg, New York

Dear Chani,

Wow! I'm just so excited! I just got a call from my folks. They were full of news. Bloomfield is quiet without us. Freydie got a new tooth. Rebbetzin Falovitz went to *Eretz Yisrael* for vacation. Morah Sherman is expecting a baby. And...I'm going to Switzerland and Israel!!!!!

My father's got business in Zurich (that's in Switzerland, in case you didn't know!) and he's going to combine it with a family vacation — and I do mean family! All of us are going together. We'll be leaving right after Yom Kippur, and then going on to Israel for Sukkos. I'm just so thrilled! The Swiss Alps — dreamy! Maybe I'll bring a sketchbook and paint them! And then *Eretz Yisrael* — the *Kosel*, *Kever Rachel*, Tzefas — I can't believe it!

You can imagine how I carried on when I found out. Typical — Chinky just kind of smiled and said she's happy, and I went nuts! I told everyone here about it, and then I just wanted to share my news with you.

Anyway — other than my news (!) camp is great. Being scenery head is working out really well, *baruch Hashem*. Even though I'd wanted it so badly, I can tell you I was a bit nervous, being the only camper among the heads, but everyone was nice and no one made me feel young or anything. I love doing my own thing. I don't know why, but when it comes to art I just hate taking orders from others.

Nothing much else is new here. Raizy and Shani are both working on a camp newspaper — just like back home — and Nechama sent away that little bird I told you about. I thought it was really brave of her to let it go and have its freedom. I must say, Nechama's changed a lot over the summer.

By the way, speaking of Nechama, she asked how Ilana Silver is doing in camp. She's sort of wondering about her, seeing as they'll be working together and all that. Drop us a line about her.

Take care, have fun, and don't forget to WRITE!

Love,

Pinky

"Here's a letter for you, Chani," Judy, junior counselor in Camp Shalva's Bunk 12A said, handing it over to her. "That's pretty stationery," she added, glancing at the floral pattern.

The petite, dark-haired girl smiled as she eagerly took the envelope. "My friend who wrote it has great taste. She's an artist," she explained.

Chani sat down on her bed, tucked her legs cozily beneath her, and prepared to read Pinky's letter. She always enjoyed hearing from her friend. Though Chani had been going to Camp Shalva for years and had many friends there, she felt just a bit disappointed that she wouldn't be with the other girls who had put out the *B.Y. Times* this year.

The *B.Y. Times*. She still could hardly believe that she — little Chani Kaufman — would be editor-in-chief of Bais Yaakov's newspaper when school began again. She sure hoped she would be able to handle it...

So what was new? Wow, Switzerland and Israel. Fabulous! Chani was really happy for her friend. And if she felt just the tiniest twinge of...was that jealousy? — after all, her parents couldn't afford a trip to Disneyworld, forget about Europe and Israel — Chani resolutely ignored it. She loved her family, and not everybody could be rich like the Chinns were. Right?

So Pinky felt "a bit nervous" about being the youngest, and the only camper, among the cantata heads. Good for her! Chani felt a lot more than "a bit" nervous about taking Shani's place as editor of the *Times*. To be perfectly honest about it, she was downright terrified!

Oh, Ilana Silver. Nechama wanted to know about her. Ilana had joined their school recently. Her parents had moved to Bloomfield from California. She'd been the surprise choice for distribution assistant, working under Nechama.

Ilana had spent the summer here in Camp Shalva. Chani, curious about her newest staff member, had kept an eye out for her, though she was three bunks below her. And now Nechama wanted to know what she thought of her.

What could she write? Ilana was...was so...so....

No, she couldn't really describe her. Not without risking *lashon hara*, that was for sure.

Nechama would just have to find out for herself.

Chani reread the letter and then prepared to answer it. She checked her calendar — Mrs. Handler had told them it was always proper to put a date on a letter. Wow! The middle of August already. That meant only three-and-a-half weeks until school started. And then it would be back to tests, to teachers...and to the *B.Y. Times*.

She couldn't wait!

**Why is Ilana Silver so indescribable?
Will Pinky come down to earth...with a thud?
And how will Chani do as editor-in-chief?
Read all about it in the next edition of
The B.Y. Times.**

You've Read About Them...
Now Write About Them!

We at **Targum Press** have been having a ball publishing the adventures of the girls who put out the *B.Y. Times*. Now we want you kids to join in the fun. Pick your favorite *B.Y. Times* characters and send us a short story about them. We'll choose the best of the stories and feature them in a future *B.Y. Times*—and you kids will be the authors!

So sharpen your pencils or plug in your computers and start writing!

Make sure you write your name on every page of the story, and your address and phone number on the first page. Send your entry to **Targum Press,** 22700 W. 11 Mile Rd., Southfield, Michigan 48034. Deadline for entries is November 15, 1992.

Have you read these other *B.Y. Times*?

☐ #1: SHANI'S SCOOP   ☐ #5: SPRING FEVER
☐ #2: BATYA'S SEARCH   ☐ #6: PARTY TIME
☐ #3: TWINS IN TROUBLE ☐ #7: CHANGING TIMES
☐ #4: WAR!   ☐ #8: SUMMER DAZE

and coming soon:

☐ #9: HERE WE GO AGAIN!   ☐ #10: THE NEW KIDS

**Once there was a family.
Their name was Baker.
They had many children.
Twelve of them.**

Baker's Dozen

The Bakers live in Bloomfield with their twelve kids—including the famous Baker quintuplets! We've got action, adventure, excitement, fun, and important lessons in this series from the people who brought you the popular *B.Y. Times.*

☐ Baker's Dozen #1: On Our Own
☐ Baker's Dozen #2: Ghosthunters!
☐ Baker's Dozen #3: And the Winner Is...

and coming soon

☐ Bakers' Dozen #4: Stars In Their Eyes
☐ Bakers' Dozen #5: The Inside Story